WITHDRAWN

Learning Resources Center
Carroll Community C...
1601 W...
Westmi...

W9-ACE-684

WITHDRAWN

The Tale of Genji

The Tale of Genji

LEGENDS AND PAINTINGS

INTRODUCTION BY **Miyeko Murase**

GEORGE BRAZILLER
New York

PUBLISHED BY GEORGE BRAZILLER, INC., IN 2001

The illustrations of the *Genji monogatari (The Tale of Genji)*
are reproduced from an album in two volumes dating from the Edo
period, seventeenth century, and executed in ink, color, and gold on paper.
Property of Mary Griggs Burke.

Photography of the Burke albums is by John Bigelow Taylor, New York.

Introduction © 2001 by Miyeko Murase
All rights reserved
First Edition

No part of this publication may be reproduced in
any form or by any means without prior
permission in writing from the publisher.

For information, please address the publisher:

George Braziller, Inc.
171 Madison Avenue
New York, NY 10016

Library of Congress Cataloging-in-Publication Data

"The tale of Genji" : paintings and legends /
introduction by Miyeko Murase.
p. cm.
54 paintings from the Burke albums "attributed to
Tosa Mitsuoki (1617–1691) . . . however, they were more
likely done by an anonymous artist of the Tosa school."
Cf. Introduction, p. 2.
Includes bibliographical references.
ISBN 0-8076-1500-5
1. Murasaki Shikibu, b. 978? Genji monogatari—Illustrations.
I. Murase, Miyeko.
II. Tosa, Mitsuoki, 1617–1691.
ND1059.6.G4 T35 2001
751.7′7′095209032—dc21   2001035321

DESIGN BY POLLEN/Stewart Cauley
PRINTED IN CHINA THROUGH ASIA PACIFIC OFFSET

Contents

Acknowledgments   *vii*

INTRODUCTION   *1*

A NOTE ON THE BURKE ALBUMS   *22*

LEGENDS AND PAINTINGS   *23*

PRINCIPAL CHARACTERS   *141*

Acknowledgments

THIS BOOK has benefited greatly from the efforts of numerous people. In particular, I would like to express my thanks to Mary Burke for her generosity in making the albums available for publication and for her unstinting support of this project. I am grateful to Mr. and Mrs. Joe Price for graciously allowing me to examine two albums of *Genji* illustrations in their collection. Stephanie Wada, Associate Curator at the Burke Foundation, read my manuscript and provided many valuable suggestions. Finally, my thanks to Mary Taveras at George Braziller, Inc., for her contribution to the expansion of the legends.

INTRODUCTION

Miyeko Murase

THE LITERARY masterpiece of Japan, *The Tale of Genji* ranks among the world's greatest works of romantic literature. This prose narrative, written early in the eleventh century during Japan's golden Heian period (794–1185), had an enormous impact on Japanese literature. Its impact on the visual arts, however, was just as great. No other Japanese text, in fact, has inspired as many works of literary illustration as *The Tale of Genji*. The very first illustrations seem to have been created shortly after the novel was written, and even today, a thousand years later, artists continue to be inspired by its compelling story.

The long history of *Genji* illustration has produced a wide range of works varying in format, iconography, medium, style, and technique. Among the traditional, standardized iconographies that inevitably evolved, the imagery that emerged from the Tosa school of painting became the most favored and most widely recognized of *Genji* illustrations. This influential school, spanning several generations, established the most familiar visual vocabulary for *Genji* illustrations. One of the finest works executed by a member of the Tosa school are the Burke albums, two albums of small, nearly miniature paintings dating from the seventeenth century. The albums contain a complete set of illustrations of the novel—one per chapter—and are in excellent condition, rare for illustrations dating from this period. These miniature paintings represent the epitome of traditional *Genji* iconography as established by the Tosa school. Delicate and refined, they capture the aristocratic sophistication of the Heian court and bring to life the events of the novel. The subtle colors exude a grace befitting the figures portrayed, and the ample use of gold ink imbues the images with a brilliant luminosity. The albums have been attributed to Tosa Mitsuoki (1617–1691), one of the school's greatest leaders; as discussed below, however, they were more likely done by an anonymous artist of the Tosa school.

As narrative illustrations, the Burke albums are inseparable from the text that inspired them. An understanding of *The Tale of Genji*, its author, and Japanese literature at the time the novel was written, as well as an understanding of the long tradition of *Genji* illustration, is essential for a full appreciation of the albums. The following brief study makes an attempt at presenting some of the more important aspects of both; it is hoped that this essay will enrich the enjoyment of those who encounter these exquisite paintings.

About *The Tale of Genji*

GENJI MONOGATARI[1] (The Tale of Genji) is one of the world's most enduring as well as one of the earliest prose narratives in the history of romantic literature. That it was written in about A.D. 1000, so early in the history of world literature, and that its author, Murasaki Shikibu, was a relatively young woman of about thirty when she wrote it, are only two of the remarkable facts about this novel. The tale is further distinguished by the complexity of its plot; the depth of its emotions; its keen observation of nature, human psychology, and social behavior; and a highly sophisticated prose style. The events the novel describes span almost three-quarters of a century and involve more than 430 characters. The English translation by Edward G. Seidensticker runs to more than 1,090 pages.[2] To think that Murasaki Shikibu composed this voluminous masterpiece without the aid of a computer!

Written in the contemporary, colloquial language of the eleventh-century court, the tale is divided into fifty-four chapters, and the text contains 795 *waka* (thirty-one-syllable poems), the vehicle through which aristocratic men and women expressed their thoughts and emotions in Heian times. Characters' names are culled from key poems in the text, which also provide evocative chapter titles. The story opens with the birth of Genji, known in later literature as "Hikaru Genji" (the shining Genji), son of an emperor by his favorite concubine. He is a man of rare physical beauty, great sensitivity and intelligence, and exceptionally cultivated taste. The narrative follows Genji's life from his youth through his meteoric rise in rank and influence, focusing above all on his numerous romantic encounters with women of varying classes, personalities, cultural achievements, and appearances—even with those of very modest beauty. At least ten ladies maintain fairly constant relationships with him throughout his life, and he has, in addition, two "official" wives, first Aoi and then the Third Princess. Seven women from Genji's circle of consorts, lovers, and wards are given the honor of lending their names to chapters of the novel: Utsusemi (Chapter 3, The Shell of the Locust), Yūgao (Chapter 4, Evening Faces), Wakamurasaki (Chapter 5, Lavender), Suetsumuhana (Chapter 6, The Safflower), Aoi (Chapter 9, Heartvine), Asagao (Chapter 20, The Morning Glory), and Tamakazura (Chapter 22, The Jeweled Chaplet). Of all these ladies, Murasaki is by far Genji's favorite. However, because of her relatively humble birth to a family of the lower aristocracy she can never become his primary wife.

After Genji's death at the age of fifty-two, the novel continues with the life of his handsome but lackluster son Yūgiri and concludes with the lives of Genji's grandson Niou and the tragic Kaoru, who passes for Genji's youngest son. The final ten chapters of the novel, which are mainly devoted to Kaoru and Niou, are commonly known as the *Uji Jūjō* (Ten Books of Uji), as many of their events are set in the rustic countryside of Uji, outside Kyōto. The superficial friendship and rivalry between the two princes is the theme of these chapters, with the plot subordinate to the psychological development of Kaoru.

Thought by all to be Genji's son, Kaoru is actually the child of a brief, tragic liaison between Kashiwagi, the son of Genji's best friend, and the Third Princess, Genji's young second wife. Kaoru is a melancholy introvert—a sort of "modern" man—regarded as literature's first antihero. Niou is his very antithesis, and his easy success with women, which forever eludes Kaoru, is drawn in sharp contrast to Kaoru's romantic struggles. Easygoing, unreliable, and somewhat shallow, Niou always achieves his goal with women, but without total emotional commitment on his part.

Genji and Murasaki, personifications of male and female virtues, are believed to have been modeled after historical personages. Murasaki Shikibu obviously derived their characteristics from the figures of society that surrounded her, shaping them according to her own concept of the ideal man and woman. Throughout the novel, Genji is depicted as a man of the utmost refinement, sensitive and quick to recognize and appreciate beauty—in nature, human emotions, the arts, colors, shapes, and fragrances. He is the symbol par excellence of the ideals valued by the cultivated court society of the Late Heian period (ca. 900–1185). Murasaki, on the other hand, represents the feminine ideal; her extraordinary beauty and grace are unequaled, as are her warm compassion, compliant nature, and refined instincts. The only discernible flaw in this otherwise perfect woman is that she is childless.

Because the *Genji monogatari* vividly reflects contemporary social mores, it is a valuable historical document as well as a great work of fiction. The ideas it expresses on the arts, the aesthetics of courtly elegance, and cultivated taste are rarely touched upon in other sources of the era. For example, in Chapter 17 (A Picture Contest), critical views are expressed on art and artistic fashion;[3] an equally astute critique on music is found in Chapter 35 (New Herbs: Part Two).[4] These statements reflect thoughts on Japanese aesthetics at a time when the Japanese were becoming increasingly conscious and proud of their indigenous artistic achievements, after centuries of looking to China for guidance in the arts.

Murasaki Shikibu

CENTURIES AFTER the *Genji monogatari* was written, a tradition developed that Murasaki Shikibu retired to a quiet retreat at Ishiyama-dera, a Buddhist temple founded in the eighth century, overlooking the beautiful expanse of Lake Biwa. According to this tradition, she had been commissioned by an empress to write a story, and she sought not only an undisturbed refuge but also an inspiration from the Buddha. An *emaki* (illustrated handscroll) depicting the history of Ishiyama-dera contains a scene of a lady, presumably the author of the *Genji monogatari*, looking over the moonlit lake on an autumn evening. This handscroll, painted by Tosa Mitsunobu (1434?–?1525), attests to the tendency, prior to and during the fifteenth century, to associate Murasaki Shikibu with Ishiyama-dera. Although the story is most likely apocryphal, it is nevertheless quite possible that Murasaki Shikibu visited the temple when she was in the service of Empress Shōshi, who undertook a pilgrimage to this temple. This event may have contributed to the creation of this legend; it is also possible that Lake Biwa, its beauty celebrated by the ancient Japanese, became linked to the author of the greatest romantic tale of ancient Japan.

Genji is clearly the work of an extraordinary talent, a keen observer of human foibles and social mores, as well as a knowledgeable critic of artistic theories. Unfortunately, much of Shikibu's life remains a mystery, as there is little extant material to inform us about her, save the fragmented remains of her memoir, the *Murasaki Shikibu nikki* (The diary of Murasaki Shikibu). Shikibu's memoir complements her novel, for it reveals not only the details—including daily activities and atmosphere—of the imperial court during her period of service but also the perceptive and probing qualities of her own mind. By piecing together facts gleaned from various sources, we know that Shikibu came from a literary family that included poets and several women authors, among them the wife of Fujiwara Kaneie (929–990), who wrote the *Kagerō nikki* (The gossamer years diary), and her niece (b. 1008), a daughter of Sugawara Takasue, who wrote the *Sarashina nikki* (The Sarashina diary). Shikibu's father, Fujiwara Tametoki, was a minor nobleman of the all-powerful Fujiwara clan and a poet as well. Her personal name may have been Takako, but this cannot be ascertained since women of the period were more often referred to by the ranks and titles held by their male kinsmen. Thus "Shikibu" may refer to the title held by her father: Shikibu no Daijō (Senior Secretary in the Bureau of Ceremonials). The origin of "Murasaki" is also unclear. The name means "lavender" and may be a reference to wisteria *(fuji)*, itself an allusion to her family name Fujiwara (meaning "wisterial field"). Or, it may derive from the name of the most important female character in the *Genji* story: Murasaki.

The year of her birth is also uncertain, but what little information there is suggests that it may have been in 970 or 978. She was apparently a bright child, but she was born during an era when evidence of superior female intelligence was no cause for special joy. According to an entry in her memoir, she memorized and recited passages from the Chinese classics, which she learned by eavesdropping on lessons given to her brother but forbidden to her because of her gender.[5] The study of Chinese literature was considered inappropriate for the delicate female sex, and Shikibu's father lamented her intellectual prowess, wishing that she had been born a boy.

She recorded in her journal the perceptions that some of her contemporaries held of her: "pretentious, awkward, difficult to approach, prickly, too fond of her tales, haughty, prone to versifying, disdainful, cantankerous, and scornful," all of which disturbed her considerably. It seems to have pleased her that those who had direct contact with her found her "strangely meek and a completely different person."[6] Around 997 she married a minor Fujiwara clansman named Nobutaka (950?–1001), who seems to have been more than twenty years her senior and already the father of five sons. She gave birth to a daughter in 999, who later became a poet of some repute under the name of Daini no Sanmi. Shikibu's marriage lasted only a few years, however, as Nobutaka died in 1001. Sometime around 1005 she began her service at the court of Shōshi, the consort of Emperor Ichijō (r. 986–1011) and the eldest daughter of the powerful Fujiwara Michinaga, archpatriarch of the Fujiwara clan.

In spite of the persistent legend that Shikibu retired to Ishiyama-dera to write her novel, it is not known exactly when she began it or what prompted her to embark on such an ambitious project. Her interest in literature from her childhood years and her wish to cope with the tedium of being a young widow and mother, of which she speaks in her memoir, may have been reasons as good as any to turn to writing. Indications are that she started her narrative before entering court life around 1005 and that by the time she began service it was well under way. According to her memoir, her novel was read aloud to Emperor Ichijō in the first month of 1009.[7] Fujiwara Michinaga also noted that there was a manuscript of her novel in the empress's possession, which would seem to suggest that the work was by 1009 more or less complete.[8]

A Look at Japanese Literature during Shikibu's Time

SHIKIBU LIVED at a critical juncture in the history of Japanese culture, and during one of the most brilliant periods in the history of Japanese literature—a period distinguished by the accomplishments of three of the greatest women writers of all time: the witty and sharp-tongued Sei Shōnagon (ca. 968–1025), who served under Teishi, Shōshi's rival at court; the passionate Izumi Shikibu (b. 976?); and, of course, Murasaki Shikibu herself. Sei Shōnagon is known for her observant, if often acerbic, remarks about people, objects, ideas, and events that fill her *Makura no sōshi* (The pillow book), while Izumi Shikibu—almost as renowned for her many love affairs as she is for her poetry—is best known for her *Izumi Shikibu nikki* (The Izumi Shikibu diary). Murasaki Shikibu must have died sometime around 1015, when her name ceases to appear in court records, several years after she is believed to have completed *Genji*.

During Murasaki Shikibu's life, almost a century after the imperial court had severed official ties with China in 894, the Japanese were gradually assimilating what they had previously borrowed from the mainland civilization. Moving away from an indiscriminate imitation of Chinese arts, the Japanese of Shikibu's time created styles in the arts that were better suited to their culture; these evolved further in later historical periods. One development that had an immeasurable impact on Japanese culture was the invention of *kana* script. Phonetic syllables derived from the cursive form of selected Chinese characters, *kana* was used to represent the separate syllables of Japanese words. It was as simple to use as a Western alphabet and enabled educated members of society to keep records in their spoken language, which differs considerably from Chinese in both grammatical structure and pronunciation. Although inadequate for official business, *kana* syllabary proved extremely effective for recording human feelings. The freedom of expression it provided was unprecedented, and it revolutionized the arts, particularly in the areas of literature, calligraphy, and painting. For the first time, poets and novelists were able to produce a vernacular literature. Without *kana*, it would have been impossible to create *waka* (thirty-one-syllable verses), many of the period's beautiful calligraphic works, and, above all, great narratives like *The Tale of Genji*.

Men were slow to appreciate the potential of *kana* and resisted moving away from literary forms and conventions borrowed from China. Their works, as a result, often lacked vision and originality. Women, on the other hand, were quick to take advantage of *kana*, most likely because they were discouraged from using the Chinese language and from studying Chinese literary classics. *Kana* was the one medium of literary expression available to them, and indeed, women virtually monopolized prose writing in *kana* script. The Late Heian period was without doubt an exhilarating period for women of letters; never before or since have women played such an important role in shaping Japanese literature.

Although Shikibu's book cannot be separated completely from the writings of her predecessors, no literary work of earlier centuries anticipated the vast scope of the *Genji* novel—a large-scale, fully developed romantic tale. The collections of short stories and *waka* that preceded *Genji* were only meek precedents hinting at the future creation of a narrative masterpiece. As early as 1200, in the early years of the Kamakura period (1185–1333), the anonymous author of the *Mumyō zōshi* (The nameless book) already recognized the significance of Shikibu's achievement and called the *Genji monogatari* a miraculous performance for a woman who had had almost nothing to draw upon from the past.

An Overview of the History of *Genji* Illustration

UNFORTUNATELY NEITHER Shikibu's holograph nor the manuscript that Michinaga saw in the empress's possession exists today. But many later copies attest to the novel's enormous popularity even outside her own court circle. One young woman, the author-to-be of the *Sarashina nikki,* noted her pleasure at receiving a copy of the *Genji* tale as a gift in 1021 when she was a girl. Not only did the tale influence innumerable literary works, it also served as a subject for painting and various decorative arts. No other written text, sacred or profane, matched the *Genji monogatari* in popularity and longevity as a subject for the visual arts. There is no doubt that the novel represents both the pinnacle of Japanese literary achievement and the primary focus for Japanese artists in the history of literary illustration. No eleventh-century *Genji* paintings—or even reference to them—exist, but the earliest records of lost *Genji* illustrations, as well as the earliest set of extant *Genji* paintings, date to the beginning of the twelfth century, roughly a century after the novel was written.

Although no actual works survive, illustrations are known to have accompanied the tales that preceded the *Genji monogatari*. Documentary evidence suggests that as early as the ninth century the practice of illustrating *waka* was quite common. Some scholars argue that the illustration of literary works was so common that early romantic tales were meant to be illustrated from their inception and that their texts were intended for recitation by one person while another listened and looked at the pictures. Such an illustrated reading is, in fact, described in Chapter 50 (The Eastern Cottage) of the *Genji monogatari*.[9]

The oldest existing *Genji* paintings, which date from the early 1100s, are among the most beautiful.[10] Only twenty-eight sections of text and twenty segments of paintings remain today, divided among various collections, with the Gotoh Museum and the Tokugawa Reimeikai Foundation, both in Tokyo, holding the largest share. The text and paintings in these fragments epitomize the sophisticated courtly style of calligraphy and painting of the period. The text comprises a nearly complete rendition of the novel and is written in elegant *kana* script on paper delicately ornamented with thin pieces of gold and silver foil cut in varying shapes and sizes. In the original handscroll, paintings alternated with text sections before the work was removed from the scrolls for protection. Episodes from thirteen chapters of the narrative are depicted in the paintings, and it appears that more than one illustration was produced for each chapter. As many as one hundred scenes might have been included in the set as it existed in its original condition.

The beauty of these *Genji* pictures remains unsurpassed. Brilliantly colored, these small compositions distill for eternity the ideals of an introspective Heian society. They re-create courtly life, with all its joys and sorrows, and the figures, though seldom shown in motion, achieve a timeless grace within the framework of the exquisite compositions.

Some of the pictorial conventions in these illustrations have been preserved for centuries. Many appear in the Burke album paintings reproduced here; for example, human figures are strictly conventionalized, without facial expression and without distinguishing characteristics in their physiognomy and gender. The figures, particularly the women, seldom stand or move about, and seated figures are completely enveloped in billowing, colorful robes. Both male and female figures have small, round faces whose features are delineated according to a technique known as *hikime-kagihana* (dashes for eyes, a hook for the nose), with thick eyebrows and tiny rosebud lips. As the text of the novel itself reiterates, long, lustrous hair was the most prized feature in a beautiful woman, and all of the ladies are shown with thick black hair streaming down their backs, reaching almost to the floor.

The very physical anonymity of these highly stylized figures allows viewers to identify themselves psychologically with the individuals portrayed in the paintings. Heian courtiers apparently read romantic tales and viewed their illustrations with an extraordinary degree of emotional involvement. A passage in the mid-tenth-century novel, the *Yamato monogatari* (The tale of Yamato), refers to a group of men and women looking at illustrations of a tale, imagining themselves as the people depicted, and composing poems about them. The absence of individuality in *Genji* figures was thus essential, as it allowed viewers to "become" the figures in the pictures. Another convention, *fukinuki-yatai* (literally, "stage with the roof blown away"), was a convenient device used to show the interiors of rooms from above, without ceiling or roof, so that viewers could have an unobstructed view of human activity within. This major pictorial convention, along with *hikime-kagihana*, survived the passage of time and was employed by artists of every historical period from the Late Heian years on, appearing in the Burke albums and other similar small-scale illustrations of the *Genji monogatari*.

The history of such a unique painting convention as *fukinuki-yatai* is not easily traced, although it is found as early as 1069 in the painting of the life of Prince Shōtoku, at the Hōryūji Temple in Nara. The origins of *hikime-kagihana* are equally difficult to pinpoint. The earliest paintings to employ the device to good effect are the twelfth-century *Genji* illustrations. However, the sophisticated and refined manner of its execution suggests that a lengthy period of evolution preceded its appearance in these works.

Very few *Genji* paintings survive from subsequent centuries until the late Muromachi period (1392–1573), in the late sixteenth century, to which a number of extant works can be dated. The majority of *Genji* illustrations from this time are delicate monochrome ink drawings, executed in the *hakubyō* (white drawings) style. Most are small handscrolls containing numerous episodes from all fifty-four chapters. Some of these charming drawings were executed by amateur female artists.

Large folding screens known as *byōbu,* usually made in pairs, and *fusuma,* sliding screens, were also vehicles for the depiction of episodes from *Genji.* A new compositional scheme was devised for these larger formats. On some pairs of six-panel screens, episodes were arranged vertically, in sequence, progressing downward from the top right corner of the right-hand screen (in accordance with the East Asian custom of reading text) and then on to the top of the second panel. This top-to-bottom, right-to-left arrangement was repeated until the far left panel on the left-hand screen was reached. Another common method of arranging *Genji* scenes on screens involved the use of only a few episodes, or even a single one, depicted in large scale. Episodes involving a large number of people, or sumptuous settings, indoors and outdoors, were generally chosen for these enlarged compositions.

Originally intended as vehicles for poems, *shikishi* (poem cards) seem to have become a major format for illustrating *Genji* late in the Muromachi period. A group of fifty-four *shikishi* bearing scenes from the novel was often pasted onto the surface of a pair of six-panel screens; this provided for easy storage and facilitated viewings by a group of people. For more intimate viewings, however, *shikishi* pasted into albums were preferred. The set of fifty-four *shikishi* in the Burke albums are themselves an excellent example of both practices. Although now mounted in two books, these small *shikishi* were most likely originally pasted on *byōbu.*

Another format for illustrating *Genji,* particularly popular in the eighteenth century, was the so-called dowry set, intended for young women about to be married. Such sets were often placed in beautiful lacquer boxes and usually consisted of fifty-four books, one volume for each chapter. The entire text of the novel was reproduced for dowry sets, while in all other sets, it was customary to copy only a selection of chosen passages from the novel. As a rule, more than one episode per chapter was chosen for illustration in these large dowry sets, expanding enormously the cycle of *Genji* illustration.

Small and inexpensive, folding fans—daily necessities in Japanese life—became popular vehicles for *Genji* pictures as well and were also produced in sets of fifty-four.

The basic iconography of *Genji* illustration was disseminated widely during the Edo period (1615–1868), providing images for a variety of media and many different types of objects. Even decorated playing cards and seashells, used in popular games, were painted with *Genji* scenes. *Genji* motifs became favorite subjects among artisans working with lacquer, metal, and textiles. Such small objects as *kozuka* (little knives) and *tsuba* (sword guards) were sometimes ornamented with a single image—a sprig or two of flowers, plants, or a bird—that had become closely associated with specific episodes of the novel. Such abbreviated images suggest that the novel, or at least some parts of it, had become familiar enough to the public to enable them to recognize such cryptic messages. For example, in the Burke albums' illustration for Chapter 4 (Evening Faces), a *yūgao* flower placed on a folding fan clearly symbolizes an episode from that chapter; insect cages represent Chapter 38 (The Bell Cricket); and ferns, Chapter 48 (Early Ferns).

Ukiyo-e wood-block prints of the nineteenth century occupy an unusual position in the evolution of the *Genji* iconography. That episodes from this classic tale should be depicted at all in ukiyo-e (pictures of the floating world) is somewhat surprising, given that this particular genre represented the plebeian world and its pleasures—a world completely removed from the aristocratic milieu and courtly aesthetic championed by the novel. Ukiyo-e artists, undaunted by the long tradition of *Genji* illustration, boldly transformed centuries-old imagery and were even so daring as to change the novel's plot. For instance, a print by Utagawa Kunisada (1786–1865) shows the rather unceremonious behavior of six women discussing some letters. This is obviously a parody of the famous episode from Chapter 2 (The Broom Tree), illustrated in the Burke albums, in which Genji and his young male friends debate the merits and virtues of women from various social classes.

Ukiyo-e artists also introduced a new pictorial treatment of this classic narrative work: women from famous *Genji* episodes were singled out and represented in solitary splendor on hanging scrolls. This was most likely inspired by the convention of individually depicting beautiful courtesans in ukiyo-e paintings and wood-block prints. Even when entirely separated from their narrative context, paintings depicting women in courtly costume and accompanied by small cats, for example, were easily recognized as representations of the Third Princess, Genji's tragic young wife, and her favorite cat, from an episode in Chapter 34 (New Herbs: Part One). Figure 1, a painting by Tsukioka Settei (1710–1786), is an example of such a painting of the Third Princess.

The most intriguing variance to evolve from traditional *Genji* illustration was the so-called *Genji Hakkei* (Eight Views from *The Tale of Genji*), inspired by the enormously popular theme of the Eight Views of the Xiao and Xiang Rivers (*Shōshō hakkei*). The famous eight vistas of the Xiao and Xiang Rivers were the best-known subject of Chinese landscape painting among Japanese ink painters from the thirteenth century on; that episodes from the *Genji monogatari,* the quintessential embodiment of classical Japanese culture, should be combined with a classical Chinese theme of poetry and painting is a testament to *Genji*'s enduring importance as a literary work and pictorial subject. *Genji* seems to have been regarded as a natural source of inspiration for scenes related to Eight Views, as it contains frequent references to changing weather, the seasons, and beautiful sites, the same aspects of nature that inspired the Chinese poems for the original Eight Views.

It is not known who first selected eight episodes from Shikibu's lengthy and complex narrative for the *Genji* Eight Views, but the oldest surviving document in which the Chinese Eight Views are combined with scenes from *Genji* is a text copied by Emperor Higashiyama (1675–1709).[11] The earliest existing set of actual illustrations may be a late-seventeenth-century rendition by the courtier Ishiyama Moroka (1669–1734) (fig. 2).[12]

Sometime before the sixteenth century, an artist (or artists) codified the many recensions of *Genji*

FIGURE 1. Tsukioka Settei (1710–1786), *The Third Princess and Her Cat,* Edo period. Hanging scroll; ink and color on silk. Mary and Jackson Burke Foundation. Photograph by Otto E. Nelson

13

FIGURE 2. Ishiyama Moroka (1669–1734), detail from Eight Views from *The Tale of Genji*.
Edo period. Handscroll; ink, color, and gold on silk.
Mary and Jackson Burke Foundation.
Photograph by Christopher Burke (Quesada/Burke Studio)

illustrations. There was evidently a need to establish a canon of textual excerpts and pictorial images to assist artists and calligraphers in creating illustrated *Genji* books and scrolls. Artists' manuals like the one in the collection of Osaka Women's College (Osaka Joshi Daigaku) in Japan appear to have been edited for this specific purpose.[13] The text of this manuscript consists of brief excerpts from the fifty-four chapters of the novel, accompanied not by paintings but by written descriptions of appropriate compositions. In other words, the manuscript was intended as a practical working model for painters and calligraphers.

The Osaka manual is a hand-copied manuscript whose calligraphic style suggests that it was written in the late sixteenth century, either during the late Muromachi (1392–1573) or the early Momoyama period (1573–1615). Although it contains the earliest extant codifications of *Genji* iconography, it was by no means the first of its kind.

Some portions of the Osaka manuscript are missing, but the lost sections were preserved in another, later version of the manual in the collection of the imperial library in Tokyo, which dates from the mid-Edo period, perhaps from the eighteenth century.

Examination of such manuals and a comparative study of *Genji* pictures of different periods reveal a distinct trend in the evolution of *Genji* illustration. The tendency was clearly to illustrate scenes that would most effectively convey the main thrust of the narrative, even in the absence of text—which is the case with the Burke albums. As the major theme of the novel is the amorous relationships of the principal characters, these are not surprisingly the most frequently illustrated scenes, followed by portrayals of festivals and ceremonies. In keeping with the traditions of Late Heian–period painting, romantic relationships were only hinted at, with very few scenes depicting men and women in actual embrace. Instead of portraying outward displays of passion, paintings show men—like Peeping Toms—spying on ladies through gaps in hedges, fences, or screens (see the illustrations for Chapters 3, The Shell of the Locust; 5, Lavender; 8, The Festival of the Cherry Blossoms; and 45, The Lady at the Bridge). The same men are depicted in pursuit of hesitant women or, more frequently, exchanging poems with them (see Chapters 30, Purple Trousers; and 47, Trefoil Knots), scenes that imply rather than state the approach of romantic involvement. The exchanging or reciting of poems appears frequently in *Genji* illustrations, as it often marked a pivotal point in romantic relationships (see Chapters 4, Evening Faces; 8, The Festival of the Cherry Blossoms; 10, The Sacred Tree; and 16, The Gatehouse). Because of the strict court protocol that kept women partially hidden behind curtains or blinds, Heian-period gentlemen were almost never able to see the ladies they pursued, even on the evening of their nuptials.[14] Lovers got to know and appreciate each other through the verses they exchanged, even before they knew what their partner looked like!

The subtle aesthetics of implication were completely abandoned in the nineteenth century in favor of more overtly passionate depictions. As we have witnessed in our own cultural history—on stage, in the cinema, and in everyday newspaper and television reportage—explicit love scenes and exaggerated expressions of grief invaded even the world of *Genji* illustrations. A nineteenth-century book of miniatures (in the Spencer

Collection of the New York Public Library) includes an extensive cycle of *Genji* pictures, three to four scenes per chapter on average, including figures shown in intimate embrace or women wailing at the death of Murasaki.

The Burke Albums

IN THE LONG history of *Genji* illustration, small *shikishi* (poem cards), like the albums reproduced here, most faithfully preserve the traditional iconography of *Genji* pictures. Averaging about six inches in height and five and one-quarter inches in width, *shikishi* produced by members of the Tosa school of painters are particularly excellent examples of traditional *Genji* iconography. The earliest example of a complete set of fifty-four *Genji shikishi*, with one picture per chapter, is, in fact, by a Tosa artist and dates from the late Muromachi period. Formerly in the Date collection in Japan, it is generally attributed to Tosa Mitsumoto (active, 1530–1569). Judging from the visible damage, the fifty-four pieces were probably pasted on screens and later removed to be remounted on album pages. Although a number of scenes in that album differ from those in the albums reproduced here, similarities in the selection of episodes are strong enough to suggest that a model book was available to generations of Tosa school artists. Neither Mitsumoto's album of *shikishi* nor the present set includes text; many similar albums, however, do contain brief passages excerpted from the novel.

Every scene in the Burke albums is framed by golden clouds at the top and bottom of the composition, giving the viewer the impression of peering in upon the events depicted through a window separating reality from the world of fiction. This conventional device, in conjunction with *fukinuki-yatai* (stage with the roof blown away) and *hikime-kagihana* (dashes for eyes, a hook for the nose), form the basis of the pictorial imagery in these delicate miniature paintings. The classical convention of *fukinuki-yatai* is particularly well suited to illustrations of *Genji* episodes, as many of the characters were essentially housebound and most of the activity takes place indoors. The high, bird's-eye point of view allows for an unobstructed view of the interiors, as in Chapter 22

(The Jeweled Chaplet). In Chapter 36 (The Oak Tree), two rooms in which simultaneous events occur are depicted in a single composition. The high viewpoint and the absence of a roof also made it possible for artists to depict indoor and outdoor scenes in the same composition, as in Chapter 10 (The Sacred Tree).

Thus exposed, room interiors and household furnishings are revealed to viewers, along with the variety of room dividers that provided privacy and protection from draft in the vast, open style of domestic architecture known as *shinden-zukuri* (literally, "bed-chamber style"). *Shinden-zukuri* was the standard architectural style used in palatial residences from the Late Heian period on. A good example appears in Chapters 3 (The Shell of the Locust) and 47 (Trefoil Knots), where semipermanent dividers, like sliding doors and black-latticed shutters installed along grooves in the floor, as well as bamboo blinds and folding screens, are depicted. Sometimes curtains suspended from lacquered poles were added to serve as temporary "walls" (see Chapter 22, The Jeweled Chaplet). These dividers often received decorative treatment. Curtains and screens are adorned with paintings, as in Chapter 38 (The Bell Cricket), most of which depict flowers and plants, although in one instance, Chapter 32 (A Branch of Plum), a landscape with geese is depicted. Wood furnishings, such as curtain poles, are lacquered in gold and black and are elaborately decorated, as book shelves also were, in a manner reminiscent of the small lacquer boxes that have survived from the Heian period.

While the hair of court noblemen was neatly coiffed and kept in place beneath tall black caps, young boys wore their long hair tied into ponytails. The very youthful Genji in Chapter 1 (The Paulownia Court) wears his long hair spread loosely over his shoulders as did girls. Ladies' long, trailing tresses, a typical mark of beauty, are painted in thick black ink, with a rich, lacquerlike sheen (see Chapter 5, Lavender). Loose strands of hair are delineated by exquisitely fine brushstrokes, as in Chapter 6 (The Safflower), believed by some scholars to have been executed with the aid of a magnifying glass—a tool introduced from Europe during the early seventeenth century.

The most striking feature of these jewel-like images is the generous use of luminous gold paint. Gold, in fact, dominates these small compositions: in addition to the clouds and ground areas, which are covered with fine gold powder, gold ink appears in the sky and water; hills, rocks, and trees are outlined or highlighted in gold, as are buildings, fur-nishings, horse trappings, and designs on clothing. The paintings literally shimmer. Silver, too, was used in depicting the moon, which once glimmered brilliantly; but, as seen in Chapters 6 (The Safflower) and 20 (The Morning Glory), for example, the color has oxidized to a grayish black. Other pigments, particularly the green used for tatami floor mats and the blue used for water, are thickly applied; both colors are sometimes combined to render rocks, with gold added for highlights. Extremely fine brushlines in black, used for hair, also define gentle waves on dark blue bodies of water.

Seasons of the year are very clearly indicated, mostly through the depiction of deli-cate plants and flowers in background landscapes. Plum and cherry blossoms signal the arrival of spring (see Chapter 8, The Festival of the Cherry Blossoms), wisteria and water lilies represent summer (see Chapter 38, The Bell Cricket), and a variety of autumnal foliage is richly rendered (see Chapter 7, An Autumn Excursion).

These features characterize the visual vocabulary of the Tosa school, which produced the images illustrated here and which preserved the traditional Japanese painting style known as *yamato-e* (literally, "Japanese painting"), over the centuries. The school's origins are traced to Tosa Yukihiro, who first used the professional name of Tosa in the early fif-teenth century. A few generations later, Mitsunobu (1434?–?1525) formally founded the school and served as the official painter of the imperial court. The turbulent years of the Momoyama period (1573–1615) were nearly disastrous ones for the Tosa school. The era's newly popular, monumental architecture demanded a novel, large-scale mode of interior decoration. Tosa artists were ill-equipped to adapt their meticulous technique to the new age which favored broadly dynamic painting styles. Consequently, Kano painters and other newly founded schools dominated the artistic arena.

Tosa Mitsuoki (1617–1691)—the artist traditionally credited with the Burke images—is revered as the master who revitalized the school in the Edo period (1615–1868), recap-turing the title of official court artist. In spite of his efforts, the Tosa studio never surpassed the all-powerful Kano school in influence and prestige.

The Burke albums are closely dependent upon the centuries-old Tosa tradition of *Genji* illustration. Their painting technique, choice of compositions, and selection of episodes for illustration reflect the canon established for *Genji* paintings by members of the Tosa school. Mitsushige (also called Mitsumochi) is the first Tosa artist whose connection with *Genji* is recorded in literature; in 1560 Emperor Ōgimachi (r. 1558–86) commissioned him to paint an episode from Chapter 9 (Heartvine) on a folding screen.[15] Mitsushige's son and pupil, Tosa Mitsumoto, is the artist to whom the earliest surviving *Genji* albums have been attributed.[16] The Mitsumoto-attributed *shikishi,* however, give only a faint hint of the miniaturist style employed for *Genji* pictures in later periods. The selection of episodes from each chapter and the composition of each scene generally follow the iconography popular among Tosa artists, suggesting that Mitsumoto used a model book. His painting style indicates that he may have been more accustomed to working on a larger scale. In his *Genji* images details of landscape and architectural settings are limited, and figures are large, imbued with energy and dynamism, virtually dominating the compositions. This style seems totally foreign to the extraordinarily refined, delicately controlled *Genji* miniatures created by later generations of Tosa artists.

Tosa Mitsuyoshi (1539–1613) is generally credited with establishing a true miniaturist style for use by the school. He was most likely a pupil of Mitsumoto, whose premature death in a military campaign of 1569 presaged a slow decline in the fortunes of the school. Mitsuyoshi's son (or pupil) Mitsunori (1583–1638) perfected the miniature style, especially in his gossamer-fine ink drawings, *hakubyō,* which he executed with astonishingly delicate brushlines. By the time Mitsunori's son Mitsuoki (1617–1691) regained the family title of official court artist, the Tosa-school approach to *Genji* illustration had been firmly standardized. Tosa illustrations are, in fact, still intimately associated in the popular mind with *Genji* paintings.

The Burke albums have traditionally been attributed to Mitsuoki, the last great leader of the school. A note pasted on the black-lacquered box in which the albums are kept identifies him as the artist. In his attempt to revitalize the artistic output of the Tosa studio, Mitsuoki introduced a degree of realism in his miniature illustrations of *Genji*. For example, in his firmly attributed *Genji* albums in a private collection in Japan,[17] gold is used sparingly: no gold appears on rocks and trees, and gold outlines were applied only occasionally on the garments of noblemen. The Burke images, on the other hand, display a lavish use of gold. Soft shades of color, particularly blue and green, help create an effect of genteel sophistication, which became a hallmark of his art. This, again, is in contrast to the Burke images, whose blues and greens are more vibrant. Figures also appear closer to the viewer than they do in the Burke albums. Most telling, however, is Mitsuoki's choice of episodes for illustration, which includes scenes not often portrayed prior to his time; they differ considerably from those depicted in the Burke collection *shikishi*.

The images featured here closely follow the standards of miniature illustrations established by Mitsuyoshi in terms of composition and painting technique—heavy application of pigments; the liberal use of gold; slender, delicate figures; and the careful delineation of minutiae in landscapes, interiors, and architecture—clearly indicating the work of an artist trained in the Tosa studio. Above all, the selection of episodes for illustration suggests the artist's strong reliance on a model of the sort that must have been made available to him in the Tosa studio. Two albums in the Shin'enkan collection in Los Angeles,[18] which are almost identical to the set in the Burke collection, point to the existence of such a model. Similar in every aspect, with the exception of slight variations in minor technical details, the Shin'enkan albums must have been done by a Tosa artist who had access to the same *Genji* model. The conservative Tosa artist who created the exquisite Burke miniatures, a contemporary of Mitsuoki's, remains anonymous.

The Burke albums, which beautifully preserve the iconography and technique of the Tosa school, pay visual tribute to one of the great literary masterpieces of Japan. Capturing for later generations the elaborate elegance of Heian court culture, these small treasures offer a vivid glimpse of a golden era from Japan's history.

NOTES

1   "In the Heian period (794–1185) the word *monogatari* meant either gibberish, idle talk, or a work of prose fiction, in the vernacular, as opposed to the learned language, which was classical Chinese, or *kanbun*." From the introduction to Haruo Shirane, *The Bridge of Dreams: A Poetics of "The Tale of Genji"* (Stanford: Stanford University Press, 1987), p. xv.

2   Murasaki Shikibu, *The Tale of Genji,* trans. with an introduction by Edward G. Seidensticker (New York: Alfred A. Knopf, 1976), 2 vols.

3   Ibid., pp. 311–12.

4   Ibid., pp. 599, 605.

5   Richard Bowring, *Murasaki Shikibu: Her Diary and Poetic Memoirs* (Princeton, N.J.: Princeton University Press, 1982), p. 139.

6   Ibid., p. 135.

7   Ibid., p. 137.

8   Ibid., p. 143.

9   *The Tale of Genji,* p. 958.

10 For good color reproductions of these pictures, see Sano Midori, *"Genji Monogatari" Emaki* (Scrolls of *The Tale of Genji*), in vol. 10 of *Meihō Nihon no bijutsu* (Treasures of Japanese art), ed. Ōta Hirotarō, Yamane Yūzō, and Yonezawa Yoshiho (Tokyo: Shōgakkan, 1981). For an English-language description of some of the paintings, see Miyeko Murase, *Emaki: Narrative Scrolls from Japan* (New York: The Asia Society, 1981), pp. 64–70.

11 A slightly later copy dating from 1768 is in the collection of Kyōto University.

12 See Miyeko Murase, *Bridge of Dreams: The Mary Griggs Burke Collection of Japanese Art* (New York: The Metropolitan Museum of Art, 2000), no. 110.

13 For an English translation of the Osaka manual, with illustrations added, see Miyeko Murase, *Iconography of "The Tale of Genji": "Genji monogatari" Ekotoba* (Tokyo and New York: Weatherhill, 1983).

14 See Chapters 6 (The Safflower) and 8 (The Festival of the Cherry Blossoms).

15 See Zoku Gunsho Ruijū Kanseikai, ed., *Oyudono no nikki* (Diary of the lady-in-waiting at Oyudono), in *Gunsho ruijū hoi* (Collected essays, supplement) (Tokyo: Zoku Gunsho Ruijū Kanseikai, 1932–34), 10 vols.

16 See Baba Ichirō, ed., *"Genji monogatari": Bessatsu Taiyō Aizōban* (Taiyō, supplement, collectors treasures) (Tokyo: Heibonsha, 1976), pp. 7–60.

17 See Akiyama Ken and Taguchi Eiichi, *Gōka Genji-e no sekai: "Genji monogatari"* (Splendid world of Genji paintings: *Genji monogatari*) (Tokyo: Gakken, 1988).

18 See Pamela Buell, *Genji: A World of a Prince, Sketch from the Tale* (Bloomington, Indiana: Indiana University Art Museum, 1982).

A NOTE ON THE BURKE ALBUMS

THE ORIGINAL illustrations are mounted in two albums, bound in accordion fashion. They did not originally appear in this format and were probably placed in the present albums during the nineteenth century. The albums are kept in a large black-lacquered box, on which is pasted a small piece of plain white paper inscribed with a note identifying the paintings as the work of Tosa Mitsuoki (1617–1691), the last Edo-period leader of the Tosa school. Each album contains twenty-seven images; the first includes the illustrations corresponding to Chapters 1 to 27, while the second contains illustrations of

FIGURE 3. Burke album cover

Chapters 28 to 54. Both albums are covered front and back with beautiful blue-and-gold brocade silk patterned with a design of stylized plum blossoms, the East Asian symbol of early spring, purity, and rejuvenation (fig. 3). A small rectangular piece of paper in light green illustrated with delicate gold clouds is pasted on the front of each album as a label for the title, which was never inscribed. The covers themselves are made from thick, stiff board, their corners protected and reinforced by open metalwork fittings in silver, ornamented with a stylized peony motif. The peony, known as the "queen of flowers" in East Asia, was a symbol of wealth and beauty.

Following the East Asian custom of reading from right to left, the book opens on the right-hand side. Each of the fifty-four illustrations (the albums do not contain any text) is mounted on a page of stiff paperboard sprinkled with delicate gold particles. Narrow strips of gold-sprinkled paper are pasted on all four sides of each picture, creating a slightly raised, protective border around the painting. Each painting measures 5 $^{13}/_{16}$ x 5 $^{3}/_{16}$ in. (14.7 x 13.1 cm), while the overall size of the album page, including the border, is 8 $^{1}/_{2}$ x 7 $^{13}/_{16}$ in. (21.6 x 19.8 cm). The pages of this book have the same dimensions as the pages of the original albums.

The painting illustrating Chapter 1 (The Paulownia Court) was mistakenly placed on a verso page, while Chapter 2 (The Broom Tree) was placed on a recto. The first two images appear here in proper sequence.

MIYEKO MURASE

LEGENDS AND PAINTINGS

Kiritsubo

THE PAULOWNIA COURT

GENJI'S MAGNIFICENCE is apparent from birth. He is "a jewel beyond compare" (p. 4),* treasured by his father, the emperor, and greatly admired by all who see him. As Genji grows, so does his beauty and grace.

At the age of seven or eight, he is introduced to a member of a Korean embassy, a wise physiognomist, from whom the emperor seeks advice about the future of his favorite son. This meeting is depicted here. The young prince, seated upon a dais, faces the Korean, while his carriage and attendants wait outside the mansion. Upon seeing the boy, the sage is astonished and remarks quietly, as though to himself, "It is the face of one who should ascend to the highest place and be father to the nation. . . . But to take it for such would no doubt be to predict trouble" (p. 14). It is later said that Genji's nickname, "the shining prince," was given to him by the wise Korean.

Heeding the words of the sage, the emperor is duly cautious about his son's future—especially since Genji lacks the essential support of his maternal relatives at court. Genji's mother, who the emperor had loved above all his consorts and who had died not long after Genji's birth, came from a lower echelon of the aristocracy. As an imperial consort of low rank, she had resided at the *Kiritsubo*, or Paulownia, court—the farthest away from the emperor's living quarters of all the consorts' residences. Mindful of the political weakness Genji has inherited from his mother, the emperor feels his son's position at court would be more secure as a commoner and formally bestows upon him the name "Genji."

It is not long before the young prince is prepared to undergo the initiation ceremonies during which he receives the cap of an adult. Still only a boy of twelve, Genji is married that same evening to Aoi, daughter of the Minister of the Left. He spends little time with his new bride, however, as his passion is reserved for his father's new love, Fujitsubo, a beautiful woman who bears a striking resemblance to Genji's mother.

* This and all subsequent quotations are from *The Tale of Genji* by Murasaki Shikibu, translated by Edward G. Seidensticker, copyright © 1976 by Edward G. Seidensticker. Used by permission of Alfred A. Knopf, a division of Random House, Inc.

Chapter 2

Hahakigi

THE BROOM TREE

NOW SEVENTEEN years old, Genji is still secretly in love with Fujitsubo, his father's favorite new consort. As a guards captain, he spends most of his time at the imperial palace and very little with his wife, Aoi.

One rainy summer evening, when the imperial palace is unusually subdued, Genji withdraws to his rooms with one of his closest friends, Tō no Chūjō. Soon joined by two young courtiers, their conversation turns to the various merits and flaws of women of different social classes. This famous scene, portrayed here, shows Genji with his three friends, while outside two attendants appear to have dozed off. This discussion convinces Genji more than ever that Fujitsubo embodies the true feminine ideal. "Through all the talk Genji's thoughts were on a single lady. His heart was filled with her. She answered every requirement. . . ." (p. 38).

The next morning, Genji sets out for Aoi's residence, where he spends most of the day. But because his route to and from her home traverses an unlucky area, Genji decides to accept an invitation from the governor of Kii to spend the night at his home. There, he becomes enamored of Utsusemi, the young stepmother of his host. That night, Genji quietly slips into her quarters and carries her off to his room. He longs to see her again, but Utsusemi is all too aware of the impropriety of such a relationship and spurns his advances when he contrives a second visit. Despondent, Genji sends her this poem: "I wander lost in the Sonohara moorlands, / For I did not know the deceiving ways of the broom tree" (p. 48). This tree was thought to vanish or change shape as one approached it.

Brief but passionate, Genji's encounter with Utsusemi introduces him to the charms of women of the middle class, debated by his friends the night before. "There had been a time when such a lady would not have been worth his notice. Yes, it had been broadening, that discussion!" (p. 62).

Chapter 3

Utsusemi

THE SHELL OF THE LOCUST

ALTHOUGH GENJI continues to pursue Utsusemi ("Shell of the Locust"), she is painfully aware of the futility of maintaining a relationship with a man of Genji's stature. The orphaned daughter of a guards officer and the wife of a much older man of modest means, Utsusemi is "ashamed of herself that she had caught the eye of a man so far above her" (p. 44); still, she can't help but feel drawn by Genji's splendor and "did not want him to forget her entirely" (p. 62).

Not easily rebuffed, Genji sends her many tender letters and attempts to see her a second and then a third time. On this third visit, depicted here, Genji secretly observes Utsusemi playing Go with her stepdaughter. The woman on the right, dressed in the white robe, may be Utsusemi.

As the women prepare to retire for the evening, Genji approaches their room. Utsusemi "sensed that something was amiss. Detecting an unusual perfume, she raised her head. . . . [S]he could see a form creeping toward her. In a panic, she got up. . . . [and] slipped from the room" (p. 53).

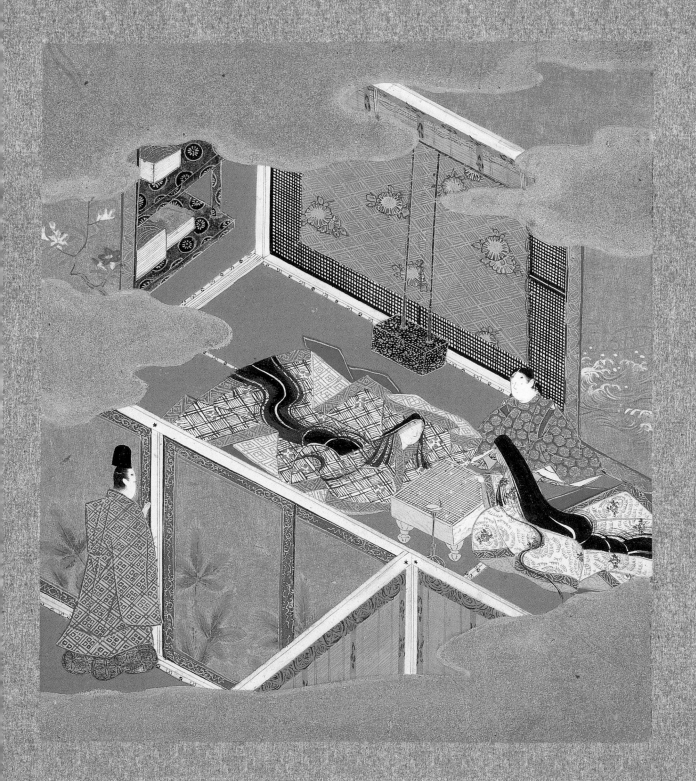

Chapter 4

Yūgao

EVENING FACES

A MAN OF deep emotion and great sensitivity, Genji stops to visit his childhood nurse, who is extremely ill. During his visit with her, he is moved to tears by the touching moment they share.

Just before entering his nurse's home, Genji notices a modest house nearby and becomes curious about its inhabitants. Intrigued, he comes closer and stops to admire the white *yūgao* ("evening faces") flowers growing over the wall. Genji requests that one of the blossoms be picked, and as shown here, it is presented to him upon a perfumed fan on which a poem has been inscribed. Thus begins Genji's brief relationship with Yūgao, the lady of the house.

His passion for her is of such intensity that when he is away from her, "his fretfulness came near anguish" (p. 66). Yearning to be with her, away from the clamor of her neighborhood, Genji brings Yūgao to an isolated villa. There, he is visited by the vengeful, jealous spirit of one of his mistresses, the Rokujō lady. The malign power of this spirit takes Yūgao's life. Genji's grief is overpowering; the last time he sees her lifeless body, he weeps over it and asks, "What was it that made me give you all my love, for so short a time, and then made you leave me to this misery?" (p. 77).

Genji later learns that Yūgao had been the mistress of his closest friend, Tō no Chūjō, and that she bore him a daughter, Tamakazura.

Chapter 5

Wakamurasaki

LAVENDER

SEEKING RELIEF from attacks of malaria that were plaguing him, Genji makes a retreat to the northern hills, where he finds the cherry trees in full blossom and a beautiful waterfall cascading into a valley. One evening, as illustrated in this painting, Genji takes advantage of the cover of haze to peer over the wattled fence of a charming house he had noticed earlier. There he spies a young girl of about ten attended by two women; she is lamenting that her favorite baby sparrows had been allowed to fly off. Genji is immediately struck by the child's promising beauty. "How he would like to see her in a few years! And a sudden realization brought him close to tears: the resemblance to Fujitsubo, for whom he so yearned, was astonishing" (p. 88). The resemblance is not a passing one: Genji later learns that the child, Murasaki ("Lavender"), is the daughter of Fujitsubo's older brother, Prince Hyōbu.

Little Murasaki is in the care of her grandmother when Genji first sees her. Almost immediately, he makes his interest in the girl known and attempts to convince the woman to put the child in his care. When the grandmother dies, Genji's hopes of having the girl are finally within sight. The night before Murasaki's father is expected to come for her, Genji arrives unexpectedly at the child's home and takes her away. She is soon installed in his palace, and though he is still deeply in love with Fujitsubo, Genji is delighted with Murasaki; "he found himself for the first time neglecting his sorrows" (p. 110).

Chapter 6

Suetsumuhana

THE SAFFLOWER

THE DAUGHTER of one of Genji's old nurses happens to mention that the late Prince Hitachi had had a daughter late in life. Genji's interest, not surprisingly, is aroused, and he convinces his nurse's daughter to sneak him into the late prince's mansion and persuade the princess, Suetsumuhana ("Safflower"), to play the koto. As planned, they meet at the mansion on a misty, moonlit spring night. Remaining out of sight, Genji listens to Suetsumuhana's playing and reflects on what must be a life of melancholy: "She had been reared in old-fashioned dignity by a gentleman of the finest breeding, and now, in this lonely, neglected place, scarcely anything of the old life remained" (p. 114).

As he is about to leave the mansion, Genji discovers that someone else is lurking about. It is his friend Tō no Chūjō, who out of curiosity followed him from the palace that evening. Here, we see the two friends together, Genji in a white formal jacket.

Although Genji finds the princess's excessive shyness trying, he is persistent. One morning, after one of his nocturnal visits, he finally chances to see her in full daylight. Her appearance is a great disappointment—she is not at all attractive. Genji continues to visit the princess despite her flaws, but it is now pity—not love—that draws him to her. Mindful of the neglect the household had fallen into after the death of Prince Hitachi, Genji takes it upon himself to attend to their needs with great care. "He resolved that he must be her support, in this not very intimate fashion" (p. 126).

Chapter 7

Momiji no Ga

AN AUTUMN EXCURSION

GENJI'S FATHER is organizing a royal excursion to the Suzaku Palace for about the middle of the Tenth Month. It promises to be a splendid affair. The emperor's most favored consort—and Genji's secret love—will not be able to attend, as she is expecting a child. Although the child is thought to be the emperor's, Fujitsubo knows it is, in fact, Genji's.

A full dress rehearsal of the excursion is held at the palace for Fujitsubo's pleasure. Tō no Chūjō and Genji perform the "Waves of the Ocean," a familiar dance. In this depiction of their performance, the young men are shown dancing beneath the leaves of a crimson maple tree. "Tō no Chūjō was a handsome youth . . . but beside Genji he was like a nondescript mountain shrub beside a blossoming cherry. . . . [Genji] seemed to shine with an ever brighter light" (p. 132).

Fujitsubo gives birth in the Second Month to a prince, and as the resemblance to Genji becomes more and more obvious, her fears and guilt intensify. "How, people asked, could someone who was not Genji yet be as handsome as Genji?" (p. 149). Surprisingly, no one—not even the emperor—guesses the truth. To secure his youngest son's position at court, the emperor names Fujitsubo empress in the Seventh Month, taking her even further beyond Genji's reach.

Chapter 8

Hana no En

THE FESTIVAL OF THE CHERRY BLOSSOMS

THE FESTIVAL of the Cherry Blossoms is held in the Grand Hall at the end of the Second Month. Genji's performance is superb. Now twenty-two, he impresses the court with his recitation of Chinese poetry and, once again, his graceful dancing.

After the festivities, Genji longs to be with Fujitsubo. Slightly drunk, he silently makes his way to her apartments but finds her door tightly closed. Disappointed yet determined, Genji attempts another route through the pavilion of Lady Kokiden, one of his father's consorts. The third door in the gallery is open, and when he approaches it, a young voice whispers sweetly, "What can compare with a misty moon of spring?" (p. 152). In this portrayal of their encounter, the young woman looks away toward her raised her fan, while Genji observes her.

Genji is immediately taken by her; "[q]uickly and lightly he lifted her down to the gallery and slid the door closed" (p. 152). Though she cannot be coaxed to reveal her identity, he suspects she is Oborozukiyo ("Night of Misty Moon"), one of Lady Kokiden's younger sisters. About a month later, through some maneuvering on his part, Genji discovers that she is, indeed, one of Lady Kokiden's younger sisters—the sixth daughter of the Minister of the Right.

Chapter 9

Aoi

HEARTVINE

AFTER GENJI'S father abdicates and the new Suzaku emperor is enthroned, Fujitsubo and the former emperor seem happier than ever. Her aloofness toward Genji continues to cause him great anguish. His many mistresses, among them the Rokujō lady, in turn complain of *his* aloofness as his growing stature forces him to be ever more discreet. These affairs are upsetting to Genji's wife and family, but as Genji doesn't lie to them, they are inclined to look the other way, especially now that Aoi ("Heartvine") is pregnant. Their joyful expectation of the coming child is unfortunately tempered with worry, as her pregnancy is a difficult one.

On the day of the Kamo Festival (celebrating the installation of a new high priestess of the Kamo Shrine), Murasaki prepares to accompany Genji to view the ceremonies. He admires her festive dress and notices that her flowing hair has not been trimmed in some time. As illustrated here, Genji takes up a pair of scissors and trims Murasaki's hair while she stands on a Go game board.

Aoi's condition, meanwhile, continues to grow worse; she "seemed to be in the grip of a malign spirit" (p. 165). Rumors that the Rokujō lady's jealous spirit is assailing Genji's wife begin to circulate, and the lady fears that it may be true, although she has never wished Aoi direct harm. At last, Aoi delivers a fine boy named Yūgiri, but sadly, she does not survive.

After a period of mourning, Genji's thoughts turn more and more to Murasaki. He decides to formally take her as his consort. "He no longer had any enthusiasm for the careless night wanderings that had once kept him busy. . . . [Mursaski] seemed peerless, the nearest he could imagine to his ideal" (p. 180).

Chapter 10

Sakaki

THE SACRED TREE

LOATHING HER own vengeful nature, the Rokujō lady is greatly pained by Aoi's death. She longs to escape the memories that haunt her in Kyōto, the capital, and decides to accompany her daughter, who has been appointed high priestess of the Ise Shrine.

As the time for her departure approaches, Genji finds the courage to visit her at the temporary shrine at Nonomiya. "Concealing himself outside the north wing, he sent in word of his arrival. . . . [T]he silence was broken only by a rustling of silken robes" (p. 186). The lady is reluctant to see him but overcomes her indecision and comes forward. Genji passes her a branch of *sakaki* (a shrub related to the camellia)—the moment illustrated here. Both are overwhelmed with memories, joyful as well as painful, and words prove

inadequate to express the full range of their emotion. They exchange a few poems and Genji departs.

More painful moments await Genji. In the Tenth Month, his father, the former emperor, dies. Although he had abdicated, he had continued to exert considerable influence at court. With the rise of a new emperor, Genji finds himself out of favor and the object of the late emperor's first wife's considerable resentment and hostility. Then, Fujitsubo announces her decision to retire from the world and take vows as a Buddhist nun. Genji has no choice but resign himself to her decision. A final blow comes when his relationship with Oborozukiyo ("Night of Misty Moon") is discovered. The scandal will later prove politically disastrous for Genji.

Chapter 11

Hanachirusato

THE ORANGE BLOSSOMS

GENJI'S TROUBLES are weighing heavily upon him. Not entirely consumed by his own worries, however, he thinks fondly of Reikeiden, one of his late father's consorts. "She had no children, and after his death her life was sadly straitened. It would seem that only Genji remembered her" (p. 215). He also remembers Reikeiden's younger sister, Hanachirusato ("The Orange Blossoms"), with whom he had had a brief affair.

One evening, he sets out to pay them a visit. Arriving at Reikeiden's apartments, Genji and she talk far into the night, sharing memories of happier times. The pleasing scent of orange blossoms drifts in from the garden, and the call of a cuckoo is heard. He later looks in on Hanachirusato. Genji is depicted here with both women.

This chapter forms a brief interlude between the events of the previous chapter (in which Genji's downfall is planned by his political adversaries) and the suffering of the next (in which their plans are carried out).

Chapter 12

Suma

THE DISCOVERY of Genji's secret affair with Oborozukiyo could not have been more damaging to his position at court. Lady Kokiden (Oborozukiyo's sister), who has harbored resentment toward Genji since his birth, takes the episode with Oborozukiyo as "a deliberate insult. She was angrier and angrier. It would seem that the time had come for her to lay certain plans" (p. 214). Genji finds himself accused of plotting against the reigning emperor by a group of courtiers faithful to the Minister of the Right (Oborozukiyo's father). The accusations, needless to say, are false, but Genji is nonetheless stripped of his exalted titles and forced into exile.

He is twenty-six when he bids farewell to those closest to him and abandons Kyōto for Suma, a coastal area to the south. In this scene, Genji and two companions watch the autumn moon and the small fishing boats in the bay. After many months of loneliness and unbearable longing to see his friends, Genji is told in a dream, "The court summons you. . . . Why do you not go? . . . Genji decided that he could stay no longer at Suma" (p. 246).

Chapter 13

Akashi

AGAIN GENJI is entreated to leave Suma in a dream. This time, it is his late father who appears to him. "And why are you in this wretched place?" he asks him. "You must leave this shore behind" (p. 250). The following morning, a monk from Akashi (actually Genji's maternal uncle) arrives and tells Genji's attendants that he had been instructed in a dream to set out in a little boat for Suma. Heeding his father's words, Genji sets off with the monk to Akashi.

Now living in the seaside town, Genji shares a delightful evening of music with the old monk. In the course of conversation, the old man confesses that he has a daughter for whom he has very high ambitions. It is clear that he hopes to interest his illustrious guest in her. Genji and the Akashi lady begin exchanging messages, and on an evening in the Eighth Month, he sets out on horseback to visit her. Genji is shown here on his way to their first meeting. "The coast lay in full view below, the bay silver in the moonlight. . . . The house was a fine one, set in a grove of trees. . . . The cypress door upon which the moonlight seemed to focus was slightly open" (p. 262). Although Genji dreads that Murasaki will learn of the affair, he doesn't wish to keep secrets from her and tells her of this latest encounter in a letter.

Back at court, there have been many changes. The Minister of the Right has died, and the emperor and Lady Kokiden have both fallen ill. Longing for Genji's return, the emperor ignores Kokiden's injunction and issues amnesty, quickly followed by a second imperial order summoning Genji back to Kyōto. His return is triumphant; he and all of those who had been expelled from court are reinstated to their former positions. One thought, however, unsettles him: he has left the Akashi lady behind, pregnant with his child.

Chapter 14

Miotsukushi

CHANNEL BUOYS

IMMEDIATELY UPON his return to the capital, Genji begins preparations for services in honor of his late father. The entire court participates in the arrangements and are reminded in the process that Genji, now twenty-eight or twenty-nine years of age, is the legitimate heir to the deceased ruler. The following year, the Suzaku emperor abdicates, and the late emperor's young son Reizei (actually Genji's son from his secret liason with Fujitsubo) is enthroned. The "causes for rejoicing were innumerable" (p. 272). All of the new emperor's supporters are promoted in rank, and Genji himself is made minister.

To express his gratitude to the gods for his brilliant return to power, Genji makes a pilgrimage to the Sumiyoshi shrine, south of Osaka. The shrine's famous curved bridge is illustrated here, as well as its torii (a gate that typically marks the approach to a Shinto shrine), and its precincts are shown teeming with Genji's attendants, all of whom are beautifully attired.

As fate would have it, the Akashi lady arrives at the shrine the very same day for her own pilgrimage. Although not included in this small composition, her boat often appears in other paintings of the scene. The splendor of Genji's entourage stuns the lady; she "felt as if she were gazing at a realm beyond the clouds" (p. 282). Ashamed of her own modest offerings, she decides to bring her boat in at Naniwa. Genji is displeased when he learns what has happened. Gazing out "over the buoys that marked the Horie channel" (p. 284) he thinks of her and sends her a poetic message alluding to the channel buoys at Naniwa. The Akashi lady's child with Genji, a girl, had been born in the Third Month.

Another of Genji's ladies, the Rokujō lady, returns from Ise. Falling suddenly ill, she asks Genji to be the guardian of her daughter, Akikonomu, just before her death. Faithful to his word, Genji brings the girl to his mansion and begins to clear the way for her presentation at court as a royal consort to the young Reizei emperor.

Chapter 15

Yomogiu

THE WORMWOOD PATCH

GENJI'S ABSENCE from the city during his exile was lamented by many ladies. None, however, lamented it more than the Safflower lady, the unattractive and impoverished daughter of the late Prince Hitachi. Since his departure, she had endured an increasingly lonely and deprived existence. The house was in a ruinous state of neglect, and her attendants had abandoned her one by one for better positions elsewhere. Despite her travails, the Safflower lady remained adamantly loyal to Genji, confident that he would remember her when he returned.

When he does finally return, the princess eagerly awaits a visit from Genji. Time is passing, however, and there is no word from him. But then one evening, when Genji is on his way to the home of the lady of the orange blossoms, he passes "a house so utterly ruinous, a garden so rank, that he almost wondered whether human beings had ever broken the wild forest" (p. 298). Overgrown with wormwood, the approach to the house is almost impenetrable. It is the princess's mansion. Here, Genji is shown making his way to the entrance, preceded by his faithful servant Koremitsu, who beats at the wet grass with a horsewhip.

Pledging her a lifetime of protection and support, Genji sees to it that the princess's every need is attended to: he sends her gifts and affectionate messages and oversees renovations to the mansion, transforming the wormwood patch into a pleasant, vibrant home.

Chapter 16

Sekiya

THE GATEHOUSE

IN AUTUMN, Genji undertakes a pilgrimage to Ishiyama. When his attendants, outfitted in fine travel livery, approach the Osaka barrier they find that an admirable party is traveling in the opposite direction. Among the party is Utsusemi, who had shared a brief romantic encounter with Genji.

In this famous scene—one of the most frequently depicted—Genji can be partly seen within his carriage as he hands a letter to Utsusemi's younger brother. "How I envy the occupant of the gatehouse. It all comes back, after years of silence," Genji writes. "I have a way of looking back upon things of long ago as if they were of this very moment" (p. 305).

The gatehouse occupant is Utsusemi's husband. The letter is to be delivered to the lady, whose carriage is just visible in the upper portion of the composition. Ever mindful of her inferior status, Utsusemi responds to Genji's letter but makes it clear that no further contact is possible.

Misfortune soon visits Utsusemi when her husband, now an old man, dies. She receives a further shock when one of his sons insinuates amorous intentions. "She could not think, were she to go on as she was, what tangles she might find herself enmeshed in" (p. 306). Deciding that it would be best to remove herself from the world, she becomes a nun.

Chapter 17

E-awase

A PICTURE CONTEST

AKIKONOMU, the Rokujō lady's daughter, had been under Genji's guardianship since her mother's death. Having carefully managed her affairs, Genji succeeds in having her presented at court as the emperor's consort. The young emperor is initially uncomfortable with his new wife but soon begins to favor her over his other lady—Tō no Chūjō's daughter—when he discovers they share a love for painting. Still, Akikonomu's position is not entirely secure. Competition grows between Akikonomu and her supporters on the one hand and Tō no Chūjo's daughter and her supporters on the other, and both sides use the emperor's love of painting to try to gain an advantage. After a time of each side's trying to outdo the other, Genji suggests a solution: why not hold a picture contest in which the final judgment is made in the emperor's presence?

"It was now the middle of the Third Month, a time of soft, delicious air, when everyone somehow seemed happy and at peace. It was also a quiet time at court, when people had leisure for these avocations" (p. 311). The day for the contest arrives. The right group (Tō no Chūjō's daughter) and the left group (Akikonomu's faction) each presents a selection of paintings; Prince Hotaru is to act as umpire and decide which selection is superior. The figures in this depiction of the contest most likely represent Prince Hotaru and the visiting Fujitsubo in the company of attending courtiers and gentlewomen. As the paintings are brought out, it is not at all clear which side will be victorious—they all seem equally impressive. Then Akikonomu's side presents it final offering: a scroll by Genji depicting life at Suma. "The assembly, Prince Hotaru and the rest, fell silent. . . . There was no point now in turning to the painting offered by the right. . . . The triumph of the left was complete" (p. 315).

Chapter 18

Matsukaze

THE WIND IN THE PINES

GENJI HAD for some time been renovating a large mansion at Nijō—the east lodge—where he plans to install various ladies. When the lodge is finally completed, Genji eagerly looks forward to the arrival of the Akashi lady and their daughter.

The lady, however, cannot bring herself to leave Akashi for the city. Because of her low rank, she foresees the humiliation and derision she could face were she to accept Genji's invitation. At the same time, she can not deny that her daughter would benefit enormously from being raised under Genji's care. A compromise is reached when her father remembers a villa on the river Oi, in a suburb of the city, that is part of the family holdings. After bidding her father a tearful, heartbreaking farewell, the lady, along with her mother and small daughter, leave Akashi and arrive at the Oi villa.

The days at Oi are long and filled with homesickness. They wait, but Genji does not come. Listening to her daughter play a strain on a koto, the Akashi lady's mother says, "I have returned alone, a nun, to a mountain village, / And hear the wind in the pines of long ago" (p. 323).

Heedless of the gossip it could generate, Genji finally leaves the city to spend two or three days with his daughter, whom he has never met. "[H]ow could she fail to be a treasure among treasures? . . . The child was a laughing, sparkling delight" (pp. 323–24). Genji's chapel and villa in nearby Katsura (which had provided him with an excuse for traveling there) takes him away from the child briefly. On the day of his return to the city, great crowds gather at Katsura, some even reaching Oi, and invite him to prolong his stay another day. As portrayed here, Genji's hosts, among them a group of falconers, present him with a sampling of their take attractively tied to autumn reeds.

Chapter 19

Usugumo

A RACK OF CLOUD

GENJI IS determined that his daughter with the Akashi lady be raised at court with all the advantages his position and wealth can provide. The lady, however, persists in her refusal to move to Nijō. Having spoken with Murasaki, who is herself childless and easily persuaded to accept the child in her household, Genji proposes that the lady turn care of the child over to Murasaki. His argument is compelling: if she herself refuses to go, then she must think of her daughter and do what is clearly best for her.

Even after the child is safely in Murasaki's care, the Akashi lady continues to be very much in Genji's thoughts. Shown here as he prepares to depart for Oi, Genji looks down at the child, who clings to his trousers. His visits to her rival continue to trouble Murasaki, but not nearly as much as before. "The little girl, scampering and tumbling about, quite filled her thoughts" (p. 357).

Meanwhile, events at court take a sorrowful turn. Aoi's father, the chancellor and Genji's father-in-law, dies. His death is soon followed by one that deals Genji an even greater blow: Fujitsubo's. Grief-stricken, Genji takes refuge in his chapel, where he spends a day in mourning. Looking out over the hills, he composes a poem: "A rack of cloud across the light of evening / As if they too, these hills, wore mourning weeds" (p. 340). Not long after Fujitsubo's funeral, her son, the Reizei emperor, makes the astounding discovery that Genji is not his half brother, but his father. Genji senses a change in the emperor's behavior, and filled with guilt, he suspects that the emperor may know the truth.

Chapter 20

Asagao

THE MORNING GLORY

GENJI HAD long been drawn to Princess Asagao, the high priestess of Kamo. When she resigns her position and returns to her late father's palace, Genji finds an excuse to visit. Her unresponsiveness merely fuels Genji's ardor, and he sends her a poem along with a morning glory. "I do not forget the morning glory I saw. / Will the years, I wonder, have taken it past its bloom?" (p. 351).

Rumors begin to circulate, and when they reach Murasaki's ears, she is at first dismissive. But then, on closer observation, she becomes concerned. The disturbing signs of restlessness in Genji's behavior cannot be ignored. To take Murasaki's mind off his frequent absences, Genji spends a day with her in her rooms. Snow had fallen throughout the day, and in the evening, he has the blinds raised so they can admire the moonlit, snow-covered garden. "Into this austere scene he sent little maidservants, telling them that they must make snowmen. Their dress was bright and their hair shone in the moonlight. . . . Rather outdoing themselves, several of them found that they had a snowball which they could not budge" (p. 357). Genji and Murasaki are shown here looking out on the garden as they discuss the various women in his life.

That night Genji dreams of Fujitsubo and awakes weeping, filled with an indescribable longing for her. The thought that she may be suffering in the afterlife is unbearable. Adding further to Genji's torments is the fear that the emperor suspects the truth about his origins.

Chapter 21

Otome

THE MAIDEN

COURT LIFE is, as usual, in a flurry of activity. Yūgiri, Genji's son with Aoi, undergoes initiation ceremonies and eventually graduates from the university after a stunning career as a student. Finally prevailing over Tō no Chūjō's daughter, Akikonomu is named empress. And there are promotions: Genji to chancellor and Tō no Chūjō to Minister of the Center.

At the harvest festival in the Eleventh Month, there are splendid performances by Gosechi dancers. They remind Genji of a dancer he was once drawn to, and he sends her note with a poem: "What will the years have done to the maiden, when he / Who saw her heavenly sleeves is so much older?" (p. 377).

Genji, now thirty-five, has outgrown his mansion at Nijō—more space is needed to accommodate his growing household. Acquiring property in Rokujō, including land once belonging to the Rokujō lady, he begins the construction of a new mansion. The four quarters of the

mansion are assigned to four ladies, each quarter designed to celebrate the beauty of one of the four seasons. The southeast quarter, reserved for Genji and Murasaki, celebrates spring; the northeast, occupied by the lady of the orange blossoms, honors summer; the northwest, future home of the Akashi lady, is given over to the austere beauties of winter; and, finally, the southwest, Akikonomu's home away from the palace, is devoted to autumn.

One evening when all but the Akashi lady had moved into the new mansion, Akikonomu sends Murasaki a gift: an ornamental box with leaves and flowers from her flourishing autumn garden arranged on the lid. The delivery of this gift is the subject of this composition. Her messenger "made her practiced way along galleries and verandas and over the soaring bridges that joined them, with the dignity that became her estate, and yet so pretty that the eyes of the whole house were upon her" (p. 386).

Chapter 22

Tamakazura

THE JEWELED CHAPLET

MEMORIES OF Genji's cherished affair with Yūgao ("Evening Faces") of many years ago are powerfully brought back to him in this fateful chapter. Ukon, one of Genji's faithful servants, makes a pilgrimage to Hatsuse, where she encounters a party with several familiar faces from years ago. They are people she knew when she was a maidservant to her much-beloved lady Yūgao. It is emotional reunion, and Ukon is overjoyed when she discovers that her lady's daughter by Tō no Chūjō, Tamakazura, is among the members of their party. Now a grown woman of twenty-one, she had been raised by her nurse and the nurse's family in Kyushu. Only recently had she returned to the capital.

Ukon wastes no time in telling Genji of her discovery. He, too, is delighted to have found her after so many years and thinks immediately of bringing her to live at Rokujō. He decides that he will say that she is his long-lost daughter; Tō no Chūjō is not to be told. After an introductory exchange of letters, preparations are undertaken without delay, and Tamakazura is moved into the Rokujō mansion. Returning from his first meeting with her, Genji composes a poem: "With unabated longing I sought the other. / What lines have drawn me to the jeweled chaplet?" (p. 405).

With the New Year quickly approaching, Genji devotes himself to the selection and distribution of festive garments among the various ladies of his household. This frequently illustrated scene portrays Genji as he examines the fine garments before him. "He would compare what the fullers had done to this purple and that red, and distribute them among chests and wardrobes, with women of experience to help him reach his decisions" (p. 406).

Chapter 23

Hatsune

THE FIRST WARBLER

IT IS NEW Year's day, and Genji sets off "for a round of calls upon his ladies" (p. 410). As he stops at each quarter of the Rokujō mansion, he finds nothing lacking—every detail is perfectly in place. He first visits Murasaki's rooms and enjoys her spring gardens. Next he stops at his daughter's rooms; her mother, the Akashi lady, has sent her New Year delicacies accompanied with a note: "The old one's gaze rests long on the seedling pine, / Waiting to hear the song of the first warbler. . . ." (p. 410). Later, Genji visits the lady of the orange blossoms in the summer quarter. From there he goes on to the rooms of the mansion's newest resident—Tamakazura's.

In the evening, Genji calls on the Akashi lady. "He was greeted by the perfume from within her blinds, a delicate mixture that told of the most refined tastes. . . .

He saw notebooks and the like disposed around an inkstone. . . . A beautifully made koto lay against the elaborate fringe of a cushion . . . and in a brazier of equally fine make she had been burning courtly incenses. . . ." (p. 412). In this rarely illustrated scene, Genji is shown looking at one of the little practice notes that lie scattered about. So taken is he with her that he decides to spend the night; his only regret is that the occupants of the other quarters will begin the New Year with pangs of jealousy.

The next day he calls on the ladies left behind at Nijō—the Safflower princess and Utsusemi, who had moved in after becoming a nun—as well as other women he has taken into his protection. Although these ladies are admittedly neglected by Genji, his attention to their needs is unfailing.

Chapter 24

Kochō

BUTTERFLIES

MURASAKI'S SPRING garden flourishes late in the Third Month. So that its beauty can be enjoyed by by the empress and her women, who are in residence at Rokujō, as well as by others at court, Murasaki and Genji plan elaborate festivities. Pleasure boats, their prows decorated with dragon and phoenix heads, carry Akikonomu's women to Murasaki's southeast quarter. Palace musicians play water music, and princes and courtiers crowd in to hear. "[E]verything about the arrangements was deliciously exotic. . . ." (pp. 418–19).

The following day, the festivities continue. Called upon to make floral offerings, Murasaki chooses "eight of her prettiest little girls to deliver them, dressing four as birds and four as butterflies" (p. 422). The delivery of her offering is depicted here. The costumed children approach the stairs with offerings of cherry blossoms and *yamabuki* flowers, a detail not shown here. Two of the pleasure boats are visible in the upper left.

The festivities over and the season now moving into summer, Tamakazura's presence is slowly becoming known. As Genji predicts, love letters begin to arrive in ever-growing numbers. Among her suitors are such important men as Prince Hotaru, Genji's widowed younger brother, as well as Tō no Chūjō's son, Kashiwagi, who is, of course, unaware that Tamakazura is his half sister. Genji himself is not immune to her charms and soon begins to make amorous advances of his own.

Chapter 25

Hotaru

FIREFLIES

GENJI'S PERSISTENT attentions shock and embarrass Tamakazura. Publicly, he behaves as her father, but privately he makes suggestive overtures. "Since she was not in a position to turn him away, she could only pretend that she did not know what was happening" (p. 430).

Genji's passion for Tamakazura does not prevent him from urging her to respond favorably to certain suitors, particularly his brother Prince Hotaru. One evening, at what seems to be Tamakazura's invitation but is really Genji's, the prince comes calling. As illustrated in this depiction of his visit, she receives him with only a curtain between them. In a moment of distraction, she suddenly notices a flash of light. Standing beside her, Genji has released fireflies from a bag. The few seconds of light are enough to reveal Tamakazura's beauty to the prince. "[T]he brief glimpse he had had was the sort of thing that makes for romance" (p. 432).

Tō no Chūjō, meanwhile, remains unaware of Tamakazura's identity. However, he often finds himself wondering about his long-lost child and regrets having had so few daughters. If she were to reappear after all these years, he is prepared to welcome her into the family.

Chapter 26

Takonatsu

WILD CARNATIONS

IT IS SUMMER, and Genji is sitting in the fishing pavilion of the southeast quarter of the Rokujō mansion trying to escape the intense heat. With him is his son Yūgiri and several of Tō no Chūjō's sons. "Though a pleasant wind was blowing, the air was heavy and the sun seemed to move more slowly than usual through a cloudless sky. The shrilling of cicadas was intense, almost oppressive" (p. 440). As illustrated here, Genji sits in a relaxed manner on a tatami mat, with the young men across from him; a trout is being prepared for an afternoon meal.

When evening falls, Genji starts toward Tamakazura's quarters; her garden is decorated with lovely wild carnations that catch the evening light. Taking out a koto, Genji plays a few notes. Her interest in the instrument is such that she soon becomes Genji's pupil, and he, of course, is delighted to have such a convenient excuse to visit her. And yet, "though he loved her very much," he knew "she would never be Murasaki's rival" (pp. 445–46).

Chapter 27

Kagaribi

FLARES

GENJI'S PASSION for Tamakazura continues unabated, but he manages to keep himself in check and display a sincere fondness for her. She, on the other hand, has overcome her initial fears and has settled in nicely at Rokujō. They spend whole days together, most of which are devoted to music lessons.

In this scene, one of the most frequently illustrated episodes from the *Tale*, Genji is shown with Tamakazura in her chambers. "He stayed very late, sighing and asking whether anywhere else in the world there were attachments quite like this one. . . . Noticing that the flares in the garden were low, he sent a guards officer to stir and refuel them" (p. 455).

Genji hears the notes of a flute and a koto being played in another wing and recognizes the playing of Yūgiri and his friend Kashiwagi. He invites them both, along with a third companion, one of Kashiwagi's brothers, to join them. Bringing along their instruments, the three young men take turns playing and singing. Tamakazura listens with knowledge that two of the young musicians are her half brothers.

Chapter 28

Nowaki

THE TYPHOON

JUST WHEN Akikonomu's autumn garden is at the height of its beauty, a severe typhoon hits, doing considerable damage to the Rokujō grounds and buildings. Amid the temporary chaos, Yūgiri catches for the first time a glimpse of Murasaki. Strict protocol, enforced by Genji throughout the years, had prevented him from ever seeing her. "Her noble beauty made him think of a fine birch cherry blooming through the hazes of spring. It was a gentle flow which seemed to come to him and sweep over him. . . . Such beauty was irresistible. . . ." (pp. 458–59).

After the storm passes, Yūgiri accompanies Genji on his calls to the various ladies in the household to inquire how they have weathered the storm. He stops in first with Akikonomu, the empress, who "had sent some little girls to lay out insect cages in the damp garden. . . . Disappearing and reappearing among the mists, they made a charming picture" (p. 462). They are, indeed, the subject of this lovely composition. During Genji's visit with Tamakazura, Yūgiri again glimpses a scene not meant for his eyes. Genji has pulled Tamakazura toward him, and "[t]hough obviously very uncomfortable, she let him have his way. They seemed on very intimate terms indeed. Yūgiri was a little shocked and more than a little puzzled" (p. 464).

After Genji's visit to the lady of the orange blossoms, Yūgiri goes to his sister's rooms (the Akashi lady's daughter). Having seen so many beauties, he is curious about how his sister would compare and hides behind a swinging door, underneath a blind. She is a charming child, with hair that does not yet reach her feet— "What a beauty she would presently be!" (p. 466).

Chapter 29

Miyuki

THE ROYAL OUTING

IN THE TWELFTH Month there is a royal outing to Ohorano, in the northwest suburb of the capital. It is splendid procession, and Tamakazura, who attends, is dazzled by the emperor. "Yes, the emperor was the best of them—though Genji so resembled him that they might have been mistaken for each other" (p. 468). Genji had naturally been invited to join the outing but excused himself as a defilement* made it impossible for him to travel. "By a guards officer the emperor sent a brace of pheasants tied to a leafy branch" (p. 469). This offering is illustrated here.

Soon after the outing, Genji decides to make Tamakazura's identity known to her father, Tō no Chūjō. He sets out to Sanjō, Tō no Chūjō's home, with the excuse of paying his ailing mother a visit. Genji and his old friend reminisce, enjoy the wine, and lament that they have not seen each other more often. When the appropriate moment presents itself, Genji tells Tō no Chūjō the truth about Tamakazura.

At Tamakazura's initiation ceremonies, Tō no Chūjō sees his daughter for the first time. "[H]e was very eager indeed to see the girl. . . . The ritual did not permit more than a glimpse of his daughter, but he could hardly keep himself from staring openly as he bestowed the train" (p. 478). An attempt is made to continue to keep Tamakazura's identity secret, but rumors inevitably spread.

---

* Some form of encounter with, or proximity to, a dead person, believed to cause temporary pollution.

Chapter 30

Fujibakama

PURPLE TROUSERS

TAMAKAZURA'S DIFFICULT position is no closer to being resolved. Genji continues to manage her affairs, despite the fact that Tō no Chūjō now knows she is his daughter, and Genji's reluctance to see her leave Rokujō prevents him from making a clear decision regarding her future. In the end, he decides that an appointment to the court position of *naishi no kami* ("wardess of the ladies' apartments") would most favor her. Even as he pursues the appointment, Genji (as well as Tamakazura) is well aware of the complications it would create. The Reizei emperor is already surrounded by women backed by either Tō no Chūjō or Genji; Tamakazura would therefore find herself in the extremely delicate political situation of competing with women sponsored by either her father or her guardian.

Meanwhile, her suitors remain as determined as ever. And their ranks are growing: now that he knows Tamakazura is not his sister, Yūgiri begins to court her openly. He makes his feelings known when Genji sends him to her quarters to convey an imperial message of welcome—her appointment has been confirmed. As shown here, Yūgiri pushes a bouquet of "purple trouser" flowers under her curtain and catches her sleeve when she reaches for it. "We may find in these flowers a symbol of the bond between us. . . . [N]ot even the august summons to court has been enough to quell my ardor" (pp. 484–85). Although Yūgiri and Tamakazura were both in mourning for the death of their grandmother, Princess Ōmiya, the artist has neglected to depict the figures in the customary gray robes, perhaps following an inaccurate model.

Chapter 31

Makibashira

THE CYPRESS PILLAR

HER APPOINTMENT to court now confirmed, Tamakazura makes a further decision: she agrees to marry Higekuro ("black beard"). Maternal uncle to the crown prince and commander of a division of the guards, he has a bright, promising future ahead of him. It's clear, however, that Tamakazura has great distaste for her new husband.

Higekuro, on the other hand, is "delirious with joy. . . . Stealing in and out of Tamakazura's rooms in the evening and morning twilight, he was the very model of youthful infatuation" (p. 492). His passionate devotion to his new wife comes at the expense of his ailing, eccentric first wife—Prince Hyōbu's eldest daughter—and his children with her. One evening, Higekuro and his first wife argue at length about the state of their marriage. It is snowing heavily, and he impatiently awaits the moment when he can slip away to be with Tamakazura. In this rarely depicted scene, Higekuro's robes are perfumed in prepara-

tion for his departure; suddenly, his wife empties the ashes from a large censer over his head, making it impossible for him to visit his new wife that evening.

The situation is clearly unbearable. Higekuro's first wife soon resolves to leave her husband and return to her father's home. One of Higekuro's children, a daughter, is heartbroken at the thought of leaving her father and her favorite seat beside the cypress pillar in the east room. "And now I leave this house behind forever. / Do not forget me, friendly cypress pillar" (p. 500).

Although now married, Tamakazura follows through with her presentation at court and proves herself superior in matters of taste and elegance after only a brief stay. As Higekuro does not want her to establish residence there, he quickly manages to whisk her away. The emperor himself sees her off regretfully.

The birth of a son in the Eleventh Month completes Higekuro's happiness.

Chapter 32

Umegae
A BRANCH OF PLUM

THE DAY OF the initiation ceremonies for the Akashi lady's daughter is approaching. Genji, now thirty-nine years old, devotes himself to seeing after every detail of the elaborate preparations. There is also her trousseau to think of, as his daughter is to be presented at court as a consort of the crown prince soon after the ceremonies. Particularly concerned about the perfumes, Genji instructs each of his ladies to prepare two blends. His brother, Prince Hotaru, is to serve as judge. "A gentle rain was falling and the rose plum near the veranda was in full and fragrant bloom. . . . [T]he brothers were admiring the blossoms when a note came. . . . It was from Princess Asagao" (pp. 512–13). The princess offers her own fragrances in two jars, as portrayed here, one decorated with a pine branch and the other with a plum branch (the artist has mistakenly decorated both jars with plum branches). All the perfumes are so pleasing that it is impossible for Prince Hotaru to select a winner.

The day of the initiation ceremonies comes and goes, as does the crown prince's own initiation. Genji's daughter is to be presented at court in the Fourth Month, and Genji now immerses himself in amassing a library for her that he "hoped would be a model for later generations" (pp. 516–17).

Watching these exciting events from afar, Tō no Chūjō feels resentful. His own daughter, Kumoinokari, remains unmarried and at home, and he begins to regret having put an end to a budding romance between her and Yūgiri. The romance has continued secretly over the years, and although Yūgiri is aware of Tō no Chūjō's regrets, he isn't prepared to give him or Kumoinokari's ladies—who had once treated him with contempt—the satisfaction of appearing eager.

Chapter 33

Fuji no Uraba

WISTERIA LEAVES

TŌ NO CHŪJŌ at last relents in his long-standing objection to Yūgiri and is prepared to accept him as a son-in-law. "Well, he had made a mistake, and that fact could not be kept secret. He must surrender and hope to do so with some dignity" (p. 523). The reconciliation would have to be handled delicately when a suitable occasion presented itself.

The moment arrives. Tō no Chūjō invites Yūgiri to a concert at his home, where he is to be the principal guest. The gathering is the subject of this illustration. The wisteria on Tō no Chūjō's veranda is in full and magnificent bloom, and judging that the moment is right, his son Kashiwagi presents Yūgiri with a beautiful spray of the flower. Reconciliation is at hand, and Yūgiri happily accepts, replying with a poem: "Tears have obscured the blossoms these many springs, / And now at length they open full before me" (p. 527). The frustrations of their thwarted courtship now over, Yūgiri is shown to Kumoinokari's rooms.

Attention shifts to Genji's daughter and her presentation at court. Murasaki was to accompany her, but only for a time. Sensing a perfect opportunity to reunite mother and daughter, Murasaki generously suggests that the Akashi lady join the girl at court. Their long separation at an end, the lady is overcome with joy and feels that her last wish is being granted.

Chapter 34

Wakana I

NEW HERBS: PART ONE

IT IS THE year of Genji's fortieth birthday, "to which the court could not be indifferent and which had long promised to send gladness ringing through the land" (p. 550). To honor him, Tamakazura arrives at Rokujō bearing a gift of new herbs that promise long life. Accompanying her are her two young sons (who had not yet been introduced to Genji), and as illustrated in this painting, they are joined by a lady-in-waiting.

The ailing Suzaku emperor begins to make preparations for his final days. Of his five children—the crown prince, who is married to Genji's daughter, and four girls—it is his third daughter that most concerns him. Determined that she have a secure life, under the protection of a dependable, admirable man, the Suzaku emperor considers many promising candidates. Despite his age, Genji emerges as the man who would make the most suitable husband (the Third Princess is herself only thirteen or fourteen at the time). He accepts, although with some reluctance, and remembers, perhaps, that the Third Princess's mother was the younger sister of Fujitsubo, the great love of his youth.

Murasaki, who is the Third Princess's cousin, feels genuinely threatened by Genji's new young wife; needlessly so, however, as Genji's disappointment in the young girl borders on the contemptuous, and his feelings for Murasaki only deepen with time. She was "more remarkable now than ever, he thought, and he had known her very well for a very long time. . . . A single morning or evening away from her and the sense of deprivation was so intense as to bring a sort of foreboding" (p. 559).

Chapter 35

Wakana II

NEW HERBS: PART TWO

TŌ NO CHŪJŌ'S son Kashiwagi had been among the candidates when the Suzaku emperor was searching for a husband for the Third Princess. Having been passed over in favor of Genji, Kashiwagi was greatly disappointed. "He still could not reconcile himself to what had happened" (p. 580).

Enjoying a beautiful spring day at the Rokujō mansion, Kashiwagi glances toward the Third Princess's rooms. A small cat suddenly runs out, and the long, tangled cord to which it is attached pulls back a curtain, revealing the Third Princess. "Seeking to calm him himself, Kashiwagi called the cat and took it up in his arms. . . . Mewing prettily, it brought the image of the Third Princess back to him (for he had been ready to fall in love)" (p. 584). Kashiwagi finds a way of borrowing the cat, and ignoring requests for its return, he keeps it by him at all times.

Years go by. Genji is now forty-six, Murasaki thirty-seven. Considered a dan-gerous year (Fujitsubo died when she was thirty-seven), Genji urges Murasaki to be especially careful. His fears are not unfounded, and she falls gravely ill the very next day. A terrifying time for Genji, Murasaki's illness presents Kashiwagi with an unusual opportunity. With practically the entire Rokujō household attending to Murasaki, who has been moved to Nijō, he knows there is not likely to be a better time for seeing the Third Princess. He had married a sister of the princess in the time since he had had his first and only glimpse of her, but he still has not been able to drive her from his thoughts. One evening, when the princess is particularly unattended, Kashiwagi is alerted. He sets out in disguise and sneaks unde-tected into her boudoir. The princess later discovers that she is pregnant. Guilt overwhelms them both, but the situation becomes truly unbearable when Genji discovers the affair.

Chapter 36

Kashiwagi

THE OAK TREE

KASHIWAGI'S GUILT devastates him. He becomes bedridden, and although his family desperately tries to help him, they remain ignorant of what is causing his mysterious illness. "I cannot face the world knowing that he knows," Kashiwagi says. "His radiance dazzles and blinds me. . . . I have so lost control of myself that it has been as if my soul were wandering loose" (p. 638).

In an attempt to find a cure for his son's condition, Tō no Chūjō consults with an ascetic knowledgeable about cures and incantations. The two men are portrayed conferring in the foreground of this painting. In another part of the house, in the upper left of the composition, Kashiwagi is talking with Kojijū, a confidant who brings him a note from the princess.

The day of the birth arrives, and the princess delivers a lovely boy, Kaoru. Her guilt, however, is overwhelming, and she repeatedly expresses her wish to become a nun. Genji hesitates but permits her to take preliminary vows. News of the birth worsens Kashiwagi's condition. Sensing that his death is imminent, he hints at what had happened to Yūgiri and asks his friend to convey his apologies to Genji; he also entrusts him with the care of his wife, the Second Princess.

"There was no one, in a world of sad happenings near and remote, who did not regret Kashiwagi's passing" (p. 656). Even Genji is sorry that such an admirable young man has died and laments most of all that he will not be able to share Kashiwagi's beautiful son with the child's grandparents.

Chapter 37

Yokobue

THE FLUTE

A YEAR HAS passed since Kashiwagi's death, and Genji, forty-nine, commissions a sutra reading in memory of the young man. "It is true that he had good reason to be angry, but the fond memories were stronger than the resentment" (p. 657).

Stopping by the Third Princess's rooms at Rokujō, Genji finds her in tears. A letter and gifts sent by her father, the Suzaku emperor, have moved her deeply. Just then, the princess's son comes into the room and totters up to a bowl of bamboo shoots sent by the retired emperor. As shown here, the boy bites into one of them. The child's beauty is startling, even more refined than his father's.

Faithful to Kashiwagi's dying request, Yūgiri occasionally stops in on the Second Princess. At the end of one such visit, the princess's mother presents him with a special gift—a flute that once belonged to Kashiwagi. That same evening Yūgiri has an unsettling dream: he and Kashiwagi are together, and taking up the flute, Kashiwagi tells him, "If it matters not which wind sounds the bamboo flute, / Then let its note be forever with my children. I did not mean it for you" (p. 663). As far as Yūgiri knows Kashiwagi has no children. Confused and remembering his friend's mysterious request that he convey his apologies to Genji for an undisclosed offense, Yūgiri pays a call at Rokujō. He tells his father about the dream and Kashiwagi's request, but Genji is evasive. Every bit as astute as Genji believes him to be, Yūgiri is not convinced by his father's answer.

Chapter 38

Suzumushi

THE BELL CRICKET

NOW FULLY devoted to religious life, the Third Princess transforms her chambers into a chapel. The entire household contributes to the effort—Genji, Murasaki, and the other Rokujō ladies—offering all kinds of riches, including brocades, covers for votive stands, incense, and robes for officiants, all of the finest workmanship. In the summer, the chapel is ready for the dedication ceremony. Looking in on the princess, Genji borrows her inkstone and, taking up a brush, writes a poem on a fan: "Separate drops of dew on the leaf of the lotus, / We vow that we will be one, on the lotus to come" (p. 669). Here, Genji is shown as he is about to begin inscribing the fan.

The Third Princess's company has grown more enjoyable to Genji since she has become a nun. He pays her frequent visits and comments during one of them on the beautiful song of the insects in her garden. "None was brighter and clearer among the insects than the bell cricket, swinging into its song" (p. 672). The evening turns into an splendid event when Prince Hotaru, Yūgiri, their attendants, and then other courtiers come calling. An invitation arrives from the Reizei palace for the entire party, and they all depart in an elegant procession to the palace. The striking resemblance between the Reizei emperor and Genji is again remarked upon, a reminder that they are father and son.

Chapter 39

Yūgiri

EVENING MIST

YŪGIRI'S VISITS with Kashiwagi's widow, the Second Princess, are on the surface a model of disinterested concern. But his feelings for the princess are of quite another nature. When the princess's mother falls ill and they both move to Ono, a suburb of the capital, Yūgiri sets off for a visit.

Resolved to finally make his feelings known, Yūgiri makes a bold move. He follows one of her ladies as she carries one of his messages back to the princess and forces his way into her presence, daring even to take her in his arms. He spends the night, and rumors begin circulating.

After the death of the princess's mother, Yūgiri continues to pursue the princess with the same determination. During a visit to Ono in the Ninth Month, he is received by one of the princess's ladies-in-waiting. Yūgiri admires the bright setting sun, the scene depicted here, and listens to the roar of the waterfall, which "was as if meant to break in upon sad thoughts" (p. 695).

Taking another bold step, Yūgiri establishes himself at Kashiwagi's former palace at Ichijo and has the Second Princess brought back from Ono. She is unyeilding, to Yūgiri's great frustration and bewilderment, but he is just at obstinate. Meanwhile, Kumoinokari, Yūgiri's wife and the mother of many of his children, is well aware of all his movements and concludes miserably that their marriage is over. Taking most of her children, she moves back to her father's house. With both his homes in complete disarray, Yūgiri asks himself, "What man in his right mind could think these affairs interesting or amusing?" (p. 710).

Chapter 40

Minori

THE RITES

MURASAKI IS dying. Increasingly weaker, she knows the end of her days is drawing near and is ready to face her death. Genji, on the other hand, "could not face the thought of surviving her by even a day" (p. 712).

In preparation, Murasaki holds elaborate religious ceremonies at Nijō. Many at Rokujō and at court participate in planning the services and in the rituals themselves. Before their conclusion, as depicted here, Murasaki and Genji enjoy the performance of a masked dancer. The beauty of the garden is such that it seems to have achieved utter perfection. Amid this joy and breathtaking beauty, Murasaki reflects on how little time she has left. She knows she will not see many people she is fond of

again, and thinking of the lady of the orange blossoms, she sends her a poem: "Although these holy rites must be my last, / The bond will endure for all the lives to come" (p. 715).

In early autumn, at the dawn of the fourteenth day of the Eighth Month, Murasaki finally expires. Genji is devastated; he has faced many sorrows but never anything of this magnitude. "It is the way of things, but it seemed more than anyone should be asked to endure. Helped to the scene by one or two of his men, he felt as if the earth had given way beneath him" (pp. 719–20). More than ever, Genji looks forward to leaving the world behind and taking religious vows.

Chapter 41

Maboroshi

THE WIZARD

GENJI REMAINS inconsolable and is pained by memories of his many romantic affairs and how they must have hurt Murasaki. Gazing up at the sky one winter evening, he wishes that she could be brought back to him. "O wizard flying off through boundless heavens, / Find her whom I see not even in my dreams" (p. 733). His one companion is his grandson Niou, whom the empress (Genji's daughter with the Akashi lady) has left with him.

A year passes, and with the early plums just coming into bloom, it is time for the ceremonial year-end prayers. In this painting, Genji is portrayed conferring with the holy man who presides over the services. Genji listens with more emotion than in the past knowing "that he would not again be present at the ceremony" (p. 734). This is one of several intimations of Genji's approaching death. Just before the year-end services, he had given his attendants gifts to remember him by and goes through his papers, burning those he would not want anyone to see. His affairs in order, Genji seems poised to leave the world behind.

Chapter 42

Nioumiya

HIS PERFUMED HIGHNESS

"THE SHINING Genji was dead, and there was no one quite like him. . . . It was as if a light had gone out" (pp. 735–36). The moment of Genji's demise is never mentioned, and when this chapter opens it is, in fact, eight years in the past. He was fifty-two. Attention now shifts fully to Kaoru and Niou, Genji's grandson.

Conceived from the tragic liason between the Third Princess and Kashiwagi, Kaoru is now twenty years old. From childhood he has been troubled by vague suspicions about his origins, but there is no one who can answer his questions. Although he reaches positions of importance at an early age and is universally admired for his handsome looks and cultivated taste, these nagging doubts hold him back, and he becomes increasingly withdrawn.

Niou, who had been Murasaki's favorite among Genji's grandchildren, is Kaoru's closest companion. They are the best of friends—as well as staunch rivals, particularly when it comes to being pleasantly perfumed (their names mean "his perfumed highness" and "the fragrant captain"). Endowed with a unique, innate fragrance, Kaoru's scent announces him wherever he goes. It also enhances other fragrances. "He used no perfume . . . but somehow a fragrance that had been sealed deep inside a Chinese chest would emerge the more ravishing for his presence" (p. 739). To compete, Niou devotes days to concocting perfumes.

At the annual New Year's archery meet the Left Guards are victorious, and the victory banquet is held at the Rokujō mansion, now under Yūgiri's care. The scene chosen for this composition depicts a procession on its way to the banquet. Both Kaoru, who had been on the losing side, and Niou ride with Yūgiri along with other high-ranking courtiers.

Chapter 43

Kōbai

THE ROSE PLUM

KŌBAI, KASHIWAGI'S younger brother and Tō no Chūjō's oldest surviving son, marries Higekuro's daughter Makibashira. It is a second marriage for both; they have both been widowed and both have children from their first marriages—Kōbai two girls and Makibashira one. Together, to Kōbai's great delight, they have a son.

As the three girls undergo initiation ceremonies, one after the other, Kōbai and Makibashira are faced with finding suitable husbands for them. Kōbai's older daughter is the first to make a match: she is given to the crown prince. For his younger daughter, Kōbai has his hopes set on Prince Niou. When his young son, an imperial page, brings him a message from Niou suggesting an interest in one of his daughters, his hopes suddenly become brighter. In response, Kōbai sends Niou a magnificent rose plum branch accompanied by a message that hints at his intentions. Here, Kōbai is shown preparing his message for Niou.

The prince's interests, however, lie with Kōbai's stepdaughter (actually a princess, daughter of Prince Hotaru)—*not* his younger daughter—and she begins to receive a steady stream of secret notes from Niou. Despite his bright prospects, Niou's attentions are not taken very seriously by Makibashira. "He was," after all, "known to be keeping up numerous clandestine liaisons" (p. 750).

Chapter 44

Takekawa

BAMBOO RIVER

TAMAKAZURA AND her marriage to Higekuro is now many years in the past. Over time, she had become very much a matron and had five children—three sons and two daughters. Higekuro has great ambitions for all of them, but then, suddenly, he dies, leaving their future entirely in Tamakazura's hands. Her sons would no doubt succeed in advancing their careers, even without the help and influence of their father; the future of her daughters, on the other hand, is much more problematic.

After long deliberation, Tamakazura decides against sending her older daughter, Ōigimi, into the service of the emperor and instead weds her to the retired Reizei emperor. Many eligible young men are disappointed, most of all one of Yūgiri's sons, who had caught a glimpse of her one spring evening when she played Go with her sister. Kaoru, too, had shown some interest in the girl. One evening late in the spring, he takes a stroll with

Ōigimi's younger brother; they stop at a pine tree they believe to be across from the new bride's curtains at the Reizei mansion. "Hanging from it was a very fine wisteria. With mossy rocks for their seats, they sat down beside the brook" (p. 765). In this painting, the young men are shown in conversation.

The fate of Tamakazura's younger daughter is still undecided. Having passed over the emperor's request for her older daughter, Tamakazura receives several indications of the emperor's displeasure. He has not forgotten that Higekuro had petitioned him to take his daughters into court service. To appease the emperor, Tamakazura maneuvers a court appointment for her daughter. "[T]he calm, dignified efficiency with which the younger sister, very handsome and very elegant, acquitted herself of her duties soon made the emperor forget his dissatisfaction" (p. 771).

Chapter 45

Hashihime

THE LADY AT THE BRIDGE

PRESENT AT A meeting between a holy man and the Reizei emperor, Kaoru is fascinated by the man's mention of one of Genji's brothers, the Eighth Prince, who lives southeast of the capital in Uji. The prince, Kaoru learns, has devoted his life to the study of Buddhism. Now twenty-two, Kaoru is himself attracted to religious life and quickly arranges a visit to Uji to meet the devout prince.

Kaoru is impressed by the intelligence and grace of the prince. The prince's two daughters—Ōigimi ("Big Princess") and Nakanokimi ("Middle Princess")—which keep him from renouncing his ties to the world, interest Kaoru, but knowing it would be inappropriate to express curiosity, he does not inquire about them.

Arriving at Uji one evening for one of his many visits, Kaoru hears the still and lonely notes of an instrument he cannot identify. The sisters are enjoying music, and Kaoru peeks in on them through an opening in a gate. "The blind had been half raised to give a view of the moon, more beautiful for the mist. . . . The princesses were farther inside. . . . It was a charming scene, utterly unlike what Kaoru had imagined from afar" (p. 785). As in many small compositions illustrating this episode, only Nakanokimi is shown with a biwa, while her sister is without an instrument. The beautiful bridge for which Uji is renowned and which is often included in depictions of this episode is not, however, included here. Reluctant to return to the city and leave the sisters, who face a lonely, isolated autumn, Kaoru sends Ōigimi a note: "Wet are my sleeves as the oars that work these shallows, / For my heart knows the heart of the lady at the bridge" (p. 790).

Aside from the prince's lovely daughters, an elderly woman in the service of the household intrigues Kaoru. He discovers that she had been one of Kashiwagi's waiting-women, and, after several interviews, she reveals to Kaoru the long-guarded secret of his birth: that Kashiwagi—not Genji—is his father.

Chapter 46

Shiigamoto

BENEATH THE OAK

NIOU HAD become increasingly curious about the Eighth Prince's daughters, about whom he had heard so much from his close companion Kaoru. When a return trip from a pilgrimage conveniently takes him in the direction of Uji, he decides to stop at one of Yūgiri's estates, just across the river from the prince's villa. Niou has musical instruments brought out, and the prince, prompted by the beautiful music he hears, sends the party a message. Unfortunately, protocol prevents Niou from calling personally on the prince as he has not been properly introduced to the family. Kaoru is therefore sent off with numerous attendants to convey Niou's response. "Summoning up all their artistry, the company played 'The River Music' as they were rowed across" (pp. 801–02). In this illustration of the crossing, the boat carrying Kaoru's party approaches the prince's home; a glimpse of one of his daughters is included in the upper right-hand corner.

The prince's worries about his daughters' future continue to trouble him. Niou has made his interest obvious, but wary of his amorous ways, the prince turns to Kaoru instead and asks him not to forget his daughters after his death. A few months later, after retiring to a nearby monastery, the prince dies. The loss is a shocking one for his daughters. "The panic, the terror, the loneliness, worse each day, were almost beyond endurance" (p. 814). Niou and Kaoru ply the princesses with letters, Niou rather more suggestively than Kaoru, both hoping that the sisters will soon emerge from their grief.

In a final scene, Kaoru once again chances upon an opportunity to spy on the princesses. The sisters are each distinguished by their own unique beauty, but it is the quieter beauty of the older daughter that Kaoru finds more compelling.

Chapter 47

Agemaki

TREFOIL KNOTS

IT IS THE anniversary of the prince's death, and Kaoru, together with the princesses, see to the general plans for the memorial service. Threads that are prepared for adorning the sacred incense inspire him to write a verse: "We knot these braids in trefoil. As braided threads / May our fates by joined, may we be together always" (p. 882).

Around this time Kaoru begins to pursue Ōigimi in earnest. Time and time again, she puts off his advances, meeting his persistence with her own equally stubborn resolve to live out her days in unworldly religious pursuits. Her only concern is her sister, Nakanokimi. "[I]f I could make a decent match for you," she tells her, "then I could tell myself I had done my duty, and it would not bother me in the least to be alone" (p. 831). Ōigimi hopes, in fact, to persuade Kaoru to shift his attentions to her sister—she is a lovely girl, and Ōigimi is certain he would not be disappointed.

Kaoru's affections, however, are not so easily transferred. During one of his visits, when he is separated from Ōigimi by only a screen, he quietly pushes it aside and, as shown in this painting, catches her sleeve as she tries to escape. It occurs to Kaoru that if Nakanokimi were matched with Niou (who has already been pursuing her), Ōigimi might become more receptive to his suit. And it would of course please Niou.

Niou and Nakanokimi *are* eventually brought together, but his infrequent visits cause the younger princess great anguish. The situation is unbearable for Ōigimi: she cannot bear her sister's unhappiness, nor can she bear the thought that she will not be able to put Kaoru off indefinitely. Her health soon begins to fail, and when Kaoru hears that she is unwell, he sees to every detail of her care. "All through the night he had women at work brewing medicines, but she quite refused to take them. He was beside himself. The crisis was real, that much was clear. And what could be done to save her?" (p. 862). She dies shortly thereafter.

Chapter 48

Sawarabi

EARLY FERNS

NAKANOKIMI IS "still benumbed with grief" over the death of her sister (p. 872). They had been as one, as Ōigimi herself had often remarked, and now, after the death of first her father and then her sister, Nakanokimi finds herself utterly alone. Karou, too, is heavy with grief. He finds his greatest consolation in Niou and a long, melancholic conversation they share one evening.

On the occasion of the New Year, the abbot from the nearby monastery in Uji sends one of Nakanokimi's women a thoughtful note accompanied with shoots of bracken and fern arranged in a basket.

The arrival of this gift is one of the most frequently illustrated and most easily identified scenes, as two baskets, holding the gifts of early spring and placed before the lady of the house, are always included in the composition.

Shortly after the New Year, Nakanokimi faces the frightening prospect of moving to the capital, where she will live in Niou's palace as his wife. "What would become of her if anything in this precarious balance should change?" (p. 882). Quite an upsetting change is, in fact, already brewing: a proposed match between Niou and Yūgiri's daughter Rokunokimi.

Chapter 49

Yadorigi

THE IVY

THE REIGNING emperor is troubled by the uncertain future faced by one of his daughters. Her mother, whom he had favored less than the empress, had suddenly died just before the princess's initiation ceremonies, leaving her alone and without significant backing at court. He decides her best option is to take a husband—and what better candidate than Kaoru?

The emperor first hints at his intentions over a game of Go. As a prize for winning the third game, the emperor invites Kaoru to break off a chrysanthemum in his garden. Kaoru is shown here with the bloom in hand. With Ōigimi still very much in his thoughts, he is not particularly eager to marry the princess. He nevertheless makes it known that he's interested, and a date for the marriage is set.

Plans for Niou's marriage to Rokunokimi are also proceeding, to Nakanokimi's great distress. Now pregnant, she is miserable at the thought of her husband taking another wife. As she grows more and more unhappy, Kaoru's sympathy for her deepens, indeed flourishes, and he regrets not having made her his when he had the opportunity. His yearning for her torments him, as does his nostalgia for Uji. On one of his visits, gazing on the sad, winter scene, he notices the ivy creeping up the mountain trees. Breaking off a sprig, he composes a verse: "Memories of nights beneath the ivy / Bring comfort to the traveler's lonely sleep" (p. 921).

The birth of Nakanokimi's child, a prince, is cause for great celebration. Kaoru, while lavish in his attentions to the new parents, laments that Nakanokimi will be even more inaccessible to him now that she is a mother. His marriage to the Second Princess is carried out with all due ceremony; his heart, however, remains in the past.

Chapter 50

Azumaya

THE EASTERN COTTAGE

RUMORS ABOUT a woman bearing a striking resemblance to Ōigimi reach Kaoru's ears. Apparently, the Eighth Prince had had a secret relationship that produced a child he refused to recognize. Kaoru is intrigued, but cautious.

The girl, Ukifune, is brought to Niou's palace and taken into the care of her half sister, Nakanokimi. Ukifune's mother has great ambitions for her beautiful daughter, and though she knows of Kaoru's interest, conveyed to her through an intermediary, she is doubtful that someone of such high stature would take a serious interest in her daughter. Nakanokimi urges her to push her doubts aside, perhaps hoping to direct Kaoru's unwelcomed attentions away from herself.

Ukifune is not quite settled in at the palace when Niou discovers her presence. Without so much as a second thought, he makes bold advances toward her. He is quickly called away by a message that his mother has taken ill, but Ukifune is left frantic. To console her, Nakanokimi invites her to her rooms and attempts to take her mind off of what has happened with illustrations to old romances. As shown here, a lady-in-waiting reads aloud to them from the accompanying texts. This scene, though well known in its twelfth-century handscroll rendition (now in the Tokugawa Museum), was seldom illustrated in post-Heian illustrations of *The Tale of Genji*.

Alarmed at Niou's behavior, Ukifune's mother removes her from the palace and hides her in a small cottage. Kaoru easily discovers the location of the house. As he waits to be received, he whispers to himself, "Are there tangles of grass to hold me back, that I wait / So long in the rain at the eaves of your eastern cottage?" (p. 966). Literally taking her up in his arms, Kaoru carries her away to Uji in his carriage.

Chapter 51

Ukifune

A BOAT UPON THE WATERS

KAORU SECRETLY installs Ukifune at the house in Uji. He would much prefer to have her nearer, but he needs time to prepare a house for her and to allow her to compose herself. Haste would only invite scandal.

Ukifune's brief encounter with Niou has meanwhile made an equally powerful impression on the prince. Despite Nakanokimi's refusal to surrender any information, he is determined to discover where and who she is. He intercepts a couple of letters from Uji, makes a few discreet inquires, and finally learns that Kaoru has a mysterious woman hidden at Uji. Setting out on a clandestine trip to Uji, Niou discovers that she is the same woman he saw at Nijō. Imitating Kaoru's voice, he cleverly steals in on Ukifune.

During a time of heavy snow, Niou visits Ukifune and carries her off to the Islet of Oranges. The most famous of all illustrations of *The Tale of Genji*, it is the scene portrayed here. As their boat approaches the shore, Niou admires the rich, long-lasting green of the pine trees. Ukifune responds with a poem: "The colors remain, here on the Islet of Oranges. / But where go I, a boat upon the waters?" (p. 991). Hidden from the world, they spend two intimate days together.

Ukifune is dazzled by Niou's considerable charm, but she cannot forget Kaoru's depth and nobility. Her dilemma becomes increasingly unbearable as both men make arrangements to bring to her to the city. "Ukifune saw doom approaching. . . . One or the other of the two men was certain to be made desperately unhappy, and the obvious solution was for her to disappear" (pp. 1005–6).

Chapter 52

Kagerō

THE DRAKE FLY

"THE UJI house was in chaos. Ukifune had disappeared, and frantic searching had revealed no trace of her" (p. 1012). The household sees now that her recent behavior had been ominous: she had burned her letters, sent poems that suggested she was contemplating suicide, and, of course, she had been so distraught over Kaoru and Niou. Her body is not found, and the only reasonable conclusion seems to be that she threw herself into the river. To avoid gossip, a hasty funeral is planned—arranged to make it appear as if there were a body—and the empty coffin is burned at the pyre.

Niou and Kaoru are grief-stricken, each in his own way, when they receive the tragic news. They each makes their own inquiries into Ukifune's last days, and Kaoru even calls on Niou, who is "indis-posed." Although they are both aware of each other's relationship with Ukifune when they meet, neither fully acknowledges it. In honor of Ukifune, Karou solemnly promises her mother to do what he can for her surviving children when they come of age to look for positions.

Both men begin to recover. Niou returns to his amorous way, while his friend indulges in minor flirtations with women at court. Kaoru, however, is tormented more than ever by his memories of Uji as well as by his reflections on the impermanence of life. Shown here deep in thought, he muses on the drake flies that flit back and forth before him one evening at Rokujō. Nowhere is the transient nature of life more obvious than in these insubstantial and fragile insects. "I see the drake fly, take it up in my hand. / Ah, here it is, I say—and it is gone" (p. 1042).

Chapter 53

Tenarai

AT WRITING PRACTICE

A SMALL party of pilgrims is forced to stop at the Suzaku emperor's villa at Uji when one of its members falls seriously ill. During their stay, they make an astonishing discovery: a weeping woman leaning against a gnarled root of a tree. Not knowing who she is nor what she is suffering from, they decide to take her back with them to Ono, to a nunnery at the west foot of Mount Hiei.

The woman is clearly Ukifune. She had intended to throw herself into the river, but, as the bishop who attends to her discovers, she had become possessed by a spirit before she could drown herself. Her recovery is slow but complete, and the people who care for her are delighted to have such a young, beautiful woman with them. Throughout her stay, Ukifune keeps her identity to herself, wanting desperately to leave her troubles behind. Over the objections of the other nuns, she herself takes vows and enters religious life. One of her few great comforts at the nunnery is her writing practice. "She seated herself at her inkstone and turned to the one pursuit in which she could lose herself when her thoughts were more than she could bear. . . ." (p. 1069). Here, Ukifune is portrayed brush in hand.

The possibility that Ukifune may be alive is eventually made known to Kaoru. He is astounded. In his usual cautious way, he lays out careful plans for discreetly seeking her out.

Chapter 54

Yume no Ukihashi
THE FLOATING BRIDGE OF DREAMS

KAORU SETS out for Yokawa on Mount Hiei to meet with the bishop there. This man had told the story of the mysterious woman discovered at Uji during a recent visit to court. The account he gives Kaoru confirms his suspicions—the woman must be Ukifune. Kaoru asks the bishop to go with him immediately to Ono to speak with her, but the bishop is reluctant. They agree, finally, to send Ukifune's little brother, whom Kaoru had taken into his service, with a letter from the bishop.

When the boy arrives at the nunnery, Ukifune continues to be evasive about her identity. In this painting, the boy waits while two women consider the letter he has brought. The nuns are angered by Ukifune's secretiveness, but they cannot persuade her to speak. "I may have known this boy when we were small," she tells them, "but please, I can't make myself try to remember. If you don't mind, I would rather let him go on thinking I am dead. . . . The gentleman the bishop speaks of: I would rather he too went on thinking I am dead" (p. 1088). Her brother carries another message from Kaoru. It is a friendly letter, but Ukifune only wants to be left alone. Crying and trembling violently, she refuses to say another word. The boy is sent off without a response.

Kaoru is greatly disappointed—his efforts have failed. Turning the matter over in his mind, he becomes suspicious: "the memory of how he himself had behaved in earlier days made him ask whether someone might be hiding her from the world" (p. 1090).

PRINCIPAL CHARACTERS

AKASHI EMPRESS

Daughter of Genji and the Akashi lady. Moved from her birthplace, Akashi, with her mother and grandmother to Oi, a suburb of Kyōto (Chap. 18, The Wind in the Pines). Later moved to Genji's household and raised by Murasaki. Consort of the reigning emperor at the end of the novel. Mother of the crown prince and Niou.

AKASHI LADY

Meets Genji at Akashi, while he is in exile, and bears him a daughter (Chap. 14, Channel Buoys). Daughter of the Akashi nun and priest. Agrees to allow Murasaki to raise her daughter (Chap. 19, A Rack of Cloud).

AKIKONOMU

Daughter of Rokujō lady and a former crown prince. Appointed priestess of the Ise shrine (Chap. 10, The Sacred Tree) and later returns to the capital (Chap. 14, Channel Buoys). Adopted by Genji when her mother dies and becomes a favorite consort of the Reizei emperor. Named empress in Chap. 21, The Maiden. First cousin of Genji and Asagao.

AOI

Daughter of the Minister of the Left and Ōmiya, a younger sister of the Kiritsubo emperor. Marries Genji (Chap. 1, The Paulownia Court) but never gains his true affection. Mother of Genji's son Yūgiri; rumored to have been killed by the jealous spirit of the Rokujō lady (Chap. 9, Heartvine).

ASAGAO

Pursued unsuccessfully by Genji, her first cousin, with whom she remains good friends throughout their lives (Chap. 20, The Morning Glory). Appointed the Kamo Priestess (Chap. 10, The Sacred Tree).

EIGHTH PRINCE

Genji's half brother and the father of Ōigimi, Nakanokimi, and Ukifune. Devoted to Buddhist study at his retreat in Uji, where he raises two of his daughters (Ōigimi and Nakanokimi). Dies in Chap. 46, Beneath the Oak.

FUJITSUBO LADY

Daughter of a former emperor. Becomes the Kiritsubo emperor's consort after the death of the Kiritsubo lady, whom she resembles. Has a secret relationship with Genji, who regards her as the ideal woman, and bears his son, the Reizei emperor (Chap. 7, An Autumn Excursion). Takes religious vows after the death of Genji's father. She dies in Chap. 19, A Rack of Cloud.

GENJI

Son of the Kiritsubo emperor. Marries Aoi, Murasaki, and the Third Princess. His secret affair with the Fujitsubo lady produces a son, the future Reizei emperor; he is also the father of Yūgiri by Aoi. Exiled to Suma and Akashi. Later returns to the capital and enjoys a brilliant return to power. Has affairs with numerous ladies including Utsusemi, Yūgao, Suetsumuhana, the Rokujō lady, the Akashi lady, and Oborozukiyo.

HANACHIRUSATO

Has a fleeting affair with Genji (Chap. 11, The Orange Blossoms). Installed at Genji's Nijō palace (Chap. 18, The Wind in the Pines) and later at the Rokujō palace (Chap. 21, The Maiden).

HIGEKURO

Most powerful man at court after Genji and Tō no Chūjō. Son of a Minister of the Right. Marries Murasaki's older sister, with whom he has two children: Makibashira (a daughter) and Tō no Chūnagon (a son). His marriage to Tamakazura (Chap. 31, The Cypress Piller) devastates his principal wife.

PRINCE HOTARU

Genji's younger brother. Serves as judge in the picture competition for the Reizei emperor (Chap. 17, A Picture Contest) and for Genji's perfume contest (Chap. 32, A Branch of Plum). Marries Makibashira, Higekuro's daughter (Chap. 35, New Herbs: Part Two).

KAORU

Son of Kashiwagi and the Third Princess, but recognized officially as Genji's son. Pursues Ōigimi, the Eighth Prince's oldest daughter, and Ukifune in vain.

KASHIWAGI

Eldest son of Tō no Chūjō, Genji's closest boyhood friend. A close friend of Yūgiri's, Genji's son. Has an illicit affair with Genji's wife the Third Princess (Chap. 35, New Herbs: Part Two), with whom he has a son, Kaoru.

KIRITSUBO EMPEROR

Genji's father; also father of the Suzaku emperor by Kokiden lady. After the death of Genji's mother, his affections shift to the Fujitsubo lady. Dies in Chap. 10, The Sacred Tree, but returns in spirit to aid Genji during his exile.

KIRITSUBO LADY

Genji's mother and the Kiritsubo emperor's favorite consort, despite her low rank. Passes away when Genji is still a young child, after enduring the jealousy and political pressure of her rivals (Chap. 1, The Paulownia Court).

KŌBAI

Tō no Chūjō's second son and Kashiwagi's brother. Marries Makibashira (Prince Hotaru's former wife) after the death of his first wife (Chap. 43, The Rose Plum).

KOKIDEN LADY

Chief consort of Kiritsubo emperor and mother of Suzaku emperor. Persecutes Kiritsubo and Fujitsubo ladies; plots Genji's downfall (Chap. 10, The Sacred Tree).

KOKIDEN NO NYŌGO

Tō no Chūjō's daughter and the Reizei emperor's consort (Chap. 14, Channel Buoys). Akikonomu's rival, with whom she holds a picture contest (Chap. 17, A Picture Contest).

KOREMITSU

Genji's faithful and constant companion. Accompanies him during his exile to Suma (Chap. 12, Suma). His son also serves Genji (Chap. 32, A Branch of Plum).

KUMOINOKARI

Tō no Chūjō's daughter. Yūgiri's childhood sweetheart; marries him in Chap. 33, Wisteria Leaves. Becomes jealous of Yūgiri's involvement with Ochiba, Kashiwagi's widow (Chap. 39, Evening Mist), and leaves him to live at her father's palace for a while.

MAKIBASHIRA

Higekuro's eldest daughter and Prince Hotaru's wife (Chap. 35, New Herbs: Part Two). Marries Kōbai after Hotaru's death.

MURASAKI

Genji's favorite consort. Fujitsubo's niece and daughter of Prince Hyōbu. Genji discovers her in Chap. 5, Lavender, and they marry privately after Aoi's death (Chap. 9, Heartvine). Childless, she raises the Akashi lady's daughter and passes away after a long illness (Chap. 40, The Rites).

NAKANOKIMI

Second daughter of the Eighth Prince of Uji and younger sister of Ōigimi. Marries Niou (Chap. 47, Trefoil Knots) and bears him a child (Chap. 49, The Ivy). Invites her half sister Ukifune to live with her (Chap. 50, The Eastern Cottage).

PRINCE NIOU

Son of the Akashi emperor. Raised by Murasaki as her favorite (Chap. 37, The Flute). Friend and rival of Kaoru. Marries Nakanokimi (Chap. 47, Trefoil Knots) and takes her to his Nijō palace (Chap. 48, Early Ferns). Later marries Yūgiri's sixth daughter, Rokunokimi (Chap. 49, The Ivy). He discovers Ukifune in Chap. 50, The Eastern Cottage, and takes her to the Islet of Oranges (Chap. 51, A Boat upon the Waters).

OBOROZUKIYO

Daughter of the Minister of the Right and younger sister of the Kokiden lady. Has a brief, scandalous affair with Genji (Chap. 8, The Festival of the Cherry Blossoms).

OCHIBA

The Suzaku emperor's second daughter. Marries Kashiwagi (Chap. 35, New Herbs: Part Two) and is widowed in Chap. 36, The Oak Tree. Yūgiri, who Kashiwagi has entrusted with her care, pursues her aggressively and marries her (Chap. 39, Evening Mist).

ŌIGIMI

Eldest daughter of the Eighth Prince of Uji. Pursued by Kaoru (Chap. 45, The Lady at the Bridge), whom she spurns and tries to match with her younger sister, Nakanokimi. She dies in Chap. 47, Trefoil Knots.

REIZEI EMPEROR

Officially the son of the Kiritsubo emperor but actually Genji's son by Fujitsubo (Chap. 7, An Autumn Excursion). Enthroned at age eleven (Chap. 14, Channel Buoys). Akikonomu is his consort (Chap. 17, A Picture Contest). Discovers the secret of his birth shortly after Fujitsubo's death (Chap. 19, A Rack of Cloud).

ROKUJŌ LADY

Mother of Akikonomu by a former crown prince, Genji's uncle. One of Genji's lovers (Chap. 4, Evening Faces). Her jealous spirit is rumored to have possessed and killed two of Genji's ladies: Yūgao (Chap. 4, Evening Faces) and Aoi, Genji's wife (Chap. 9, Heartvine). She leaves for Ise with her daughter (Chap. 10, The Sacred Tree) and later returns to the capital, where she dies (Chap. 14, Channel Buoys).

ROKUNOKIMI

Yūgiri's sixth daughter by Koremitsu's daughter (Chap. 39, Evening Mist); marries Niou in Chap. 49, The Ivy.

SUETSUMUHANA

Daughter of the deceased Prince Hitachi. Unattractive but courted by both Genji and Tō no Chūjō (Chap. 6, The Safflower). Joins Genji's household at his Nijō palace (Chap. 15, The Wormwood Patch).

SUZAKU EMPEROR

Eldest son of the Kiritsubo emperor (Chap. 1, The Paulownia Court) by the Kokiden lady. Pardons exiled Genji (Chap. 13, Akashi) and persuades him to marry his daughter, the Third Princess (Chap. 34, New Herbs: Part One).

TAMAKAZURA

Daughter of Tō no Chūjō and Yūgao (Chap. 2, The Broom Tree). Raised in Kyushu and returns to Kyōto as a grown woman (Chap. 22, The Jeweled Chaplet). Installed in Genji's Rokujō palace as his daughter but is secretly pursued by him (Chap. 24, Butterflies). Meets her father for the first time in Chap. 29, The Royal Outing. Marries Higekuro (Chap. 31, The Cypress Pillar).

THIRD PRINCESS

Third daughter of the Suzaku emperor by the Fujitsubo consort (half sister of the earlier Fujitsubo lady). Marries Genji as a young girl (Chap. 34, New Herbs: Part One) and pursued by Kashiwagi (Chap. 35, New Herbs: Part Two). She gives birth to Kashiwagi's son, Kaoru, in Chap. 36, The Oak Tree.

TŌ NO CHŪJŌ

Genji's close childhood friend and rival. The brother of Genji's wife Aoi. Has a brief affair with Yūgao and fathers Tamakazura (Chap. 2, The Broom Tree); also the father of Kokiden no nyōgo, who competes with Genji's adopted daughter Akikonomu for the Reizei emperor's affection, and of Kumoinokari, Kashiwagi,

and Kōbai. Passes away about the same time Genji does (Chap. 41, The Wizard).

UKIFUNE

Daughter of the Eighth Prince of Uji and half sister of Nakanokimi and Ōigimi, who she resembles. Is moved briefly to Nakanokimi's quarters at Niou's palace (Chap. 50, The Eastern Cottage), where she is discovered by Niou. She is pursued by both Kaoru and Niou (Chap. 51, A Boat upon the Waters). Decides to kill herself (Chap. 52, The Drake Fly) but is unsuccessful and becomes a nun (Chap. 53, At Writing Practice).

UTSUSEMI

The wife of an older man (the governor of Iyo), she has a brief affair with Genji (Chap. 2, The Broom Tree). Meets Genji by chance at the Osaka barrier on her return from the province where her husband was in service (Chap. 16, The Gatehouse). After the death of her husband, she takes holy vows and joins Genji's household at his Nijō palace (Chap. 23, The First Warbler).

YŪGAO

Has an affair with Tō no Chūjō and bears him a daughter, Tamakazura. Also has an affair with Genji. She dies suddenly, possessed by an evil spirit believed to be the Rokujō lady's (Chap. 4, Evening Faces).

YŪGIRI

Genji's son by Aoi (Chap. 9, Heartvine) and Kashiwagi's close friend. Marries his childhood sweetheart, Kumoinokari (Chap. 33, Wisteria Leaves), and later Princess Ochiba, Kashiwagi's widow (Chap. 36, The Oak Tree). His second marriage causes his first wife much pain and jealousy, but he manages to divide his time between the two women (Chap. 42, His Perfumed Highness).

ND
1059.6
G4
T35
2001   The tale of Genji.

$45.00

DATE			

WITHDRAWN

ND
1059.6
G4   **CARROLL COMMUNITY COLLEGE LMTS**

The tale of Genji.

00000009383316

Learning Resources Center
Carroll Community College
1601 Washington Rd.
Westminster, MD 21157

NOV 20 2001   BAKER & TAYLOR